About the Author

I authored sixteen textbooks and an editor asked if I had a novel in me. This unearthed a revelation… when a scientist restricted to science-fact is released to flirt with science-fiction, interesting things start to happen. My character needed a tech so I developed a solution that modeled too well, leading to a start-up, fifty patents, and acquisition by a Fortune 500. I would live out many parts of 'The Collective' as if a future echo came to call, and if my mind was read, it would be impossible to distinguish what is my principal character James and what is Nigel.

The Collective

Nigel Cook

The Collective

Olympia Publishers
London

www.olympiapublishers.com
OLYMPIA PAPERBACK EDITION

Copyright © Nigel Cook 2023

The right of Nigel Cook to be identified as author of
this work has been asserted in accordance with sections 77 and 78 of
the Copyright, Designs and Patents Act 1988.

All Rights Reserved

No reproduction, copy or transmission of this publication
may be made without written permission.
No paragraph of this publication may be reproduced,
copied or transmitted save with the written permission of the publisher,
or in accordance with the provisions
of the Copyright Act 1956 (as amended).

Any person who commits any unauthorised act in relation to
this publication may be liable to criminal
prosecution and civil claims for damage.

A CIP catalogue record for this title is
available from the British Library.

ISBN: 978-1-80439-405-2

This is a work of fiction.
Names, characters, places and incidents originate from the writer's
imagination. Any resemblance to actual persons, living or dead, is
purely coincidental.

First Published in 2023

Olympia Publishers
Tallis House
2 Tallis Street
London
EC4Y 0AB

Printed in Great Britain

Dedication

To my wife, Alonna.

Acknowledgements

Thank you, Dawn, for the hours. And thank you, Irene, for the guidance.

Chapter 1

The weather's forces at play combined constructively to generate a storm just south of Lyon in France, which tracked for over three hundred kilometers to the northeast before losing its strength at the foothills of the Swiss Alps. The mountain features around Lake Geneva channeled the storm into a swirling mass which pummeled the town and forested slopes. Rain and hail came down in sheets, sweeping over the deep, cold lake setting up sizable waves which buffeted up against a sheer natural rock base supporting an elegantly turreted medieval château. This castle had a courtyard with cylindrical towers in each corner and was surrounded by a natural moat connected to the land by a drawbridge permanently lowered and paved for cars.

Two men dressed in dark suits crossed a sentry walkway pierced with medieval arrow slits, their flashlights playing from left to right, and then entered a central residence whose facade was adorned with large, gothic windows. The expansive room had stone-arched beams extending to the full height of the ceiling, and a fire blazed in a hearth, occupying an entire wall. Recognizing the woman warming herself in a winged chair by the fireside, they skirted around a large banqueting table and waited in silent obedience.

"Fetch the prisoner, and bring him to the infirmary observation room."

"Yes ma'am", replied the lead operative.

Hannah's voice was deep, she was fine-boned and slender.

Her face was lined, had a porcelain paleness, and her white-blonde hair was slicked back in a severe style. She was wearing a masculine, grey flannel suit with high heels, and one could glean from the irritation in her tone and demeanor that she was reading a disagreeable message on her smartphone.

Deep down in the Castle-Keep, the conditions were miserable. James Moore sat on a folding camp bed in a circular dungeon without a door or windows - an oubliette, or forgotten room. The rising damp and the cold had managed to find their way in, but after several exhaustive and ultimately fruitless efforts, he had given up hope of ever finding his way out. The basic necessities were lowered in and taken out twice a day through an access hole, high in the arched ceiling. His long, lank hair and overgrown beard were of no particular color, neither brown nor fair, and he was broad-shouldered and solidly built. Only in his mid-thirties, this forced incarceration for several months had aged him. Hearing a noise from above, he looked up, revealing his blue eyes and a deep cleft in the center of his chin on a handsome face.

Shackled hand and foot, he shuffled along between the two operatives and was led into a viewing room with a large window from waist-height to the ceiling. This window afforded a clear view of a vintage infirmary with a stainless-steel operating table in the center of the room, under surgical spotlights, and a sterilizer steaming surgical instruments was alongside it. Double doors opened and in walked a nurse helping a pregnant woman into the room and onto the table, where two orderlies restrained her. Recognizing Helen, James lunged forward but was immediately restrained by his guards. Also in her early thirties, Helen was attractive, fair with pale blue eyes and a petite figure with a basketball-size baby bulge. She spasmed in pain when a contraction peaked and struggled in a state of semi-conscious sedation. Two prepped doctors entered and after the usual preliminaries, they began a cesarean section.

Hannah entered the room, seemed to intentionally take up a position to block James' view, and attached a microphone to her lapel. "Can you hear me, Mr. Moore?"

James ignored her, still vying for a better position while the senior guard holding James nodded to Hannah in acknowledgment.

"Your stubbornness has left us little choice. You seem to care very little for yourself, so let us see how much you care for those you love."

The doctor mumbled something from behind and Hannah covered the microphone to respond. In time, the nurse brought a child forward, wrapped in a swaddling blanket, and offered it to Hannah who rejected the idea out of hand.

"Congratulations, Mr. Moore, you have a son!"

As Helen whimpered in the background, Hannah frowned at the cold stare and silence from James. They were locked in a battle of wills and neither moved a muscle. When Helen let out a plaintive cry, James faltered, and finally, he gave consent with his eyes only.

"Good. In the meantime, your son will remain in the care of a guardian."

Chapter 2

Eight months earlier...

James jogged along a cliff path, clean-cut in a loose shirt, shorts, and worn trainers listening to his exercise playlist which he was convinced vastly improved his stamina. An early morning summer rain before daylight had drenched the coastal town of St. Clements and so the ground was spongy, there was a smell of damp earth, and the leaves on the trees drooped and dripped. The low grey clouds that had obscured the dramatic cliffs and coves of the Devon coast had been swept away at dawn to blend into the sea on the distant horizon.

Leaving the turquoise and teal-colored sea behind him, he could still hear the rollers thumping against the beach as he darted down a country lane lined with an ancient lichened stone wall, holding dairy cows being herded in for their morning milking.

A noted scientist and published research professor with many patents to his name, he had lived and worked in Southern California for several years before returning to his hometown in Southern England, and he couldn't help but consider the stark contrast. It was less like another country, and more like another planet. Rudely, in his view, England had not stood still in his absence and he found his native land much changed on his return. Like all expatriates, he had preserved his English customs and practices only to find the English had moved on without any regard for tradition. London was almost unrecognizable, but as he traveled away from this epicenter of England, time appeared to reverse and he was greatly relieved to find St. Clements untouched by progress. Showing his American wife, Helen, all of his old haunts had brought back feelings of almost unbearable nostalgia.

James had privately developed a Mind Link technology while in San Diego which had inadvertently made him privy to a secret that several influential parties were hell-bent on concealing at any cost. James and Helen had left in a hurry, several lives had been lost and they were lucky not to be among that number.

He was pulled out of this reflection by someone calling his name and turned to see Mr. Warder-Bond who owned the local newsagent.

"I have your newspaper James," he said, handing it to him.

Confused at it having not been delivered, he said, "Oh, thank you."

"Paperboy didn't show up again - can't get good help these days!" This was delivered with a wink. "I always knew you'd go far."

James had been a paperboy as a lad and was thought of so highly by Mr. Warder-Bond that he had entrusted him to run the shop in the early morning before going off to school. His kind words of encouragement had had a profound influence on encouraging him to believe in himself.

"Too kind, sir... they were good times," he said, placing a hand on his shoulder as he noticed with sadness how much older he now looked. "I could come back if you need me?"

"I couldn't afford you now!" he called out with a laugh, as James gave a farewell wave.

Continuing down the high street he passed the village shop,

the post office, the bank that looked like a private residence, and then turned up North Street to reach his home. It was a sizable three-story detached Edwardian house on a few acres, and, although it looked large, the impression you got was that of an unpretentious country house. Passing through the open gates, he walked the driveway to cool down, skipped up the terraced steps to the front door, and entered.

Within, it was spacious but the proportions were just right to make you feel at home. Slipping off his shoes he went straight through to the kitchen.

"Good morning, Maria," he said, kissing a lady on her cheek as she prepared breakfast.

A short Hispanic woman of indeterminate age, she was plump and matronly with a kind and gentle expression. Waving him off affectionately, and in a thick Spanish accent, she said, "Oh, Mr. James, tell 'elen to hurry, she will miss 'er train."

Taking a bottle of water from the refrigerator, he took a swig, leaving their conversation behind. Bounding up the stairs two at a time, he turned at the top and walked down the hallway to enter a brightly lit and spacious bedroom suite. Helen appeared from the bathroom, hair, and makeup done. Partially dressed in heels, a tight skirt, and a black bra with her hands held up, fingers extended, she blew on newly-painted nails. She was petite, blonde, sexy-looking, and in her early thirties, and as she spoke, you could hear her American accent. "You have to help me, James. Take off this bra and help me put on the white one there on the bed, and my blouse."

Reaching for the front clasp, he released it, registered her vulnerability, and smiled. Immediately assessing his intent, she quickly tried to muster stern authority.

"No, James, no... I have to get to work."

Removing her bra slowly and letting it drop, neither broke eye contact that was full of love and humor. Her unconvincing look of reproach melted to one of desire and in sudden abandon, she pulled off his T-shirt in one fell swoop, pushed him back onto the bed, climbed on top of him, and they kissed passionately.

***

An aide holding the hand of a seven-year-old autistic girl walked into an empty hexagonal-shaped room which looked like the inside of a beehive. It was a magical kingdom where the soundproofed spongy coated walls glowed with soft colors, encouraging a sense of peace and relaxation.

High above, a diagonal panel made of one-way glass concealed an observation room perfectly situated to view the room. A nervously pacing director circled in the center of the room, monitoring four-seated engineers, each with an array of displays, keyboards, and control panels. He was a short, balding man and was trying with every fiber of his being to will the desired result. As he paused to watch the autistic girl and her aide, he appeared to be awaiting a requirement, and, all at once, exploded with exaggerated enthusiasm.

"We're there, we're there! Input is in the hive. Activate the bubble and bring her hologram online."

A clear hexagonal-shaped enclosure, with a custom recliner within it was lifted from below the floor, lit up, and a hologram showed an ever-changing variety of revolving three-dimensional shapes of different colors hovering over the armrests.

The child was captivated by these and she climbed into the recliner.

"Activate chair massager and aromatherapy

diffusers…what's her favorite?"

The assigned engineer facing this room answered. "Rosemary fragrance."

"Okay, wait… wait… now, begin receptive conditioning sequence."

The holographic projections collapsed, and a flat screen attached to a robotic arm lifted up and took a position directly in front of the child. Displaying a DaVinci painting in brilliant color, she stared at it in a vacant way, turning her head at an incline, and a second robotic arm presented a touch-sensitive artistic pad. The girl picked up the attached stylus, selected a brush-stroke type and color on the pad's soft-key options palette, and began to copy the picture. It became quickly apparent that it would be a flawless reproduction. Her eyes reflected the liquid-like replica of the renaissance picture, and she appeared to be scanning, almost dissecting, the picture from left to right, top to bottom, pixel by pixel, for hue, value, and saturation.

Chapter 3

James waited in the driveway, car running, ready to drive Helen to the train station. He was listening to the news but turned it off as soon as she appeared with Maria in tow. Going to the wrong side of the car, she stopped abruptly at seeing James, shook her head smiling with embarrassment, and moved to the other side climbing in.

"Will I ever get used to this? Will we make it, James?"

With a smile, he said, "We'll be fine, Helen... loads of time."

Maria handed in a bag. "Eat dis on the train, 'elen."

"I will, Maria, and thank you!"

Maria closed the passenger door and they were off. The driveway was lined with trees and the spring sunlight filtered through to dapple the windshield as the wheels crunched over the gravel. Helen was redoing her nails.

"I thought you were busy today?"

"No, I finished the math book manuscript and emailed it... nothing now until production starts."

"Are you sure you don't want to take a research position? It might interest you."

"Not right now... too much association."

"Maybe in time... Oh, before I forget, Aunt Rose called. She wanted to see you."

"Ok, I'll pop in on the way home. Are you busy today?"

"Three appointments, and an emergency trauma case... a nine-year old girl, lost both parents in a car accident."

Pulling up outside the station, he exited quickly to open her door. Helen got out and in silence, they took each other's hands smiling sadly at a recollection.

"She's in good hands, Helen."

Leaning in, she kissed him lovingly, and waved farewell, saying, "I'll text you to tell you the train I'm coming back on."

"Right you are… Have a good day, my love!"

***

After James' father had died in an accident when he was thirteen, his mother had remarried planning to emigrate to Australia. Not really having a motherly disposition, and not wanting to be encumbered by a child in her new life, she had suggested he go to live with his father's sisters. Rose and May had readily accepted this unusual arrangement as they were well aware of her limitations and feared for him being unwanted and unloved. James knew his mother was just not the maternal type, a bit like some people could not cook to save their life.

World War II had sabotaged the lives of Rose and May. Aunt May had had a childhood sweetheart and there was a promise between them but he had been lost on a convoy mission in the Atlantic early in the war. Aunt Rose had managed to get a little farther along, but not by much. She and Gerald had agreed to marry impulsively to gain some certainty during the uncertainty of war, and had had a one-day honeymoon which was cut short by the D-Day invasion where he was killed on the beach. It had seemed only logical they should live together in the family home, and there they had stayed all their lives.

Crossing the town square, he turned up a small lane and parked alongside a thatched cottage adjacent to the fourteenth-century church. Feeling for the latch, he opened the wrought iron gate and walked up the rosebush-lined flagstone path to the tiny door with mullioned glass. Knocking, he heard a shout from within, "Come on in, James, it's open."

The hallway walls were paneled, but this could hardly be seen for the paintings which covered almost every square inch. The polished floors had a Persian rug runner and two flights of heavily carpeted stairs led to the upper landing where a window let in the bright morning light. A heavenly smell of baking came from the kitchen where an unseen Aunt May called out, "Go on through James, you're just in time for elevenses."

James entered a comfortable sitting room, with low oak-beamed ceilings and a large bay window seat facing the ocean. A thick Turkish rug covered most of the stone floor and against the far wall, warmth emanated from a failing coal fire in a fireplace with blackened ornate ironwork and a simple over-mantle on which were a variety of family photos. In the center of the room was an old mahogany coffee table and grouped around this were two armchairs and a comfortable old damask sofa. Two heavily-ladened bookcases had been built into alcoves on either side of the fireplace and the walls were again, densely covered with a variety of oil paintings.

A gray-haired woman with spectacles on the end of her nose sat at an easel, studying a cloud. She was small in stature, but you quickly sensed she had keen wisdom and sharp intellect. On hearing him enter, she removed a rag from her paint-covered tunic to wipe her hands and met James who leaned down to have his head clasped and to be kissed on both cheeks.

"Come and sit down, May should have coffee for us soon."

"I could murder a cup."

Aunt May walked in, searching for James, who rose from his

chair to be kissed. In contrast, she was a full-bosomed, solid-framed woman with surprisingly thin legs. She had a more practical air about her and taking an unnecessarily circuitous route around the easel, pictures, stacks of papers, and books, she picked up a full cup of cold coffee from the desk.

"I don't know why I bother; you never drink it."

Breaking from her chat with James, Rose said, "What was that, dear?"

Polishing a small section of the desk with her apron, May said, "I was just saying, it's such a waste of milk and sugar."

"You timed it perfectly, James. Just in time for coffee."

"Actually, we've already had our elevenses, but I'll make you a cup... you look a little thin, James, did you have breakfast with Helen?"

"We missed breakfast, I'm afraid, something rather pressing came up."

May scolded, "James, that poor girl. She's skinny enough as it is."

"I'd love a cup of earl gray, if you don't mind, May, with a slice of lemon, please," requested Rose.

"Of course, sister dear."

Reaching for a letter on the desk, Rose adjusted her spectacles. "I got a reply from my friend at the Ministry of Defense. Peter Blaine is still alive, although not too lucid."

"I'm sorry, Aunt Rose, I'm not following you."

"Ah yes, I'm sorry, I sensed Helen was reluctant to tell you. This is about that little black book she gave me."

James was unable to censor his shifting feelings, and his demeanor became pensive.

Rose looked on tolerantly. "Is this to do with her father?"

"Yes... and no."

"It never ceases to amaze me how clear and concise you can be when you want to, and how muddled you can be whenever this subject is broached... I'm told by my friend that it's an old Nazi code."

May entered the room with a tray. "I baked some shortbread, so help yourself." Sensing the atmosphere, she left without another word.

"He was elected governor of California, I understand?" asked Rose. "Helen believed his influence doesn't reach across the Atlantic."

"Too self-absorbed is more likely... Can you trust this friend in the ministry?"

"Implicitly... is it her father's book?"

"No."

"Peter Blaine was one of the enigma code breakers at Bletchley Park... he's in a nursing home now just outside Alton, in Hampshire."

"Please, believe me, Aunt Rose, when I tell you we need to drop this... there are malevolent forces out there you don't want unleashed."

Chapter 4

It was early evening in New York and the clouds had been threatening all day, but they timed their downpour perfectly to drench home-bound commuters as they funneled down Sixth Avenue. Rolling thunder confirmed there was no end in sight and the wet streets appeared shiny, reflecting all manner of lights, while uptown traffic sparred with horns and hollers.

A middle-aged man in a classic suit and heavy overcoat shielded his head with a newspaper as he hurried down the steps to the subway. Shaking the rain off his newspaper, he swiped his pass across the reader and passed through the turnstile heading down the escalator. Standing near the platform edge, he peered into the tunnel impatiently, and seeing and hearing nothing, continued reading.

A young woman standing behind a pillar appeared to be as keenly interested in the train, but on closer inspection, her focus was instead on the man reading. The school uniform initially placed her at high-school age, but on second glance, this ensemble put her more in her mid-twenties as it did not meet any standards of regulation. The plaid-pleated skirt had too short a hemline, the crisp button-up shirt was unbuttoned to show too much bust and the tie and badged blazer was too flamboyant. She had big eyes and a fair complexion, and she finished off this preppy private school fashion statement with pink Pom-Pom hair ties and heels. She was speaking into her cell phone and had a faint French accent. "Wait… wait… wait… wait… wait…"

A rumble was heard from the tunnel and the man leaned out past the platform edge to see the approaching train.

"Now!" she said sharply.

At that instant, the man's cell phone rang. He pulled it from his pocket and checked the caller ID before answering. For a split second, he appeared dumbstruck, and then his mouth opened, his eyes went vacant, his legs buckled, and his whole body slumped. As he collapsed, he tumbled into the rail-bed to the disbelief of onlookers who either watched in shock or turned their heads as the body was first carried, and then mangled and cut into two by the wheels riding over the rail.

***

The Alton House nursing home was originally a private residence, and, typical of the Victorian mansions of its time, it was an eclectic design of Victorian gothic, Dutch baroque and Tudor architectural styles. It was quite close to Jane Austen's home in Chawton, which James and Helen had planned to visit after meeting Peter Blaine.

As they waited for the administrator, they looked at the residents sitting in a comfortable lounge either socializing, quietly reading, or napping. Catching James' eye, Helen frowned slightly, and James shook his head. "You risk upsetting the status quo."

She looked at him tolerantly. "Don't be cross, James. Surely, forewarned is forearmed?" She laughed conspiratorially, and he inclined his head, smiling at her.

The door opened, and a short, portly, and balding man emerged. Looking at James, he asked, "Dr. Thompson?"

Helen stepped forward. "That would be me. This is my

assistant, James."

James bit his tongue, looking at Helen as she enjoyed his discomfort.

"My name is Jeremy Hickling, chief administrator."

"Thank you for taking the time to see me."

Gesturing for them to follow, he explained as he led the way.

"Peter Blaine was a brilliant mathematician and engineer who, along with every other gifted academic at that time, was recruited to break Nazi Germany's enigma code. They worked night and day for nearly four years and I'm afraid it took a heavy toll on him. He's trapped in that time, tormented by unsolved problems."

Going through to a dining area, residents were at tables sipping tea, eating cakes, chatting, and gossiping quite happily for the most part. Continuing, they passed through to a TV room which was playing *Three Days of the Condor* and exited out through French doors to a bright conservatory where residents lounged on recliners, looking out at beautifully manicured grounds.

Hickling continued, "For many years, he was kept isolated by the secret service, but most of what he was privy to no longer comes under the official secrets act. I don't know if you'll get much from him. Here he is."

Peter Blaine was in his early eighties, thin, with piercingly blue eyes that stared forward as he muttered, tapping a clenched fist against his forehead.

Helen took a seat beside him. "Mr. Blaine, my name is Helen."

He appeared to be unaware of her presence as he mumbled, "Daisy chain the relays for ten levels, but loading would be a problem, the source voltage would be pulled low, a twenty-four-volt system, maybe, the sink current would be very high."

Repositioning herself, she tried again. "I spoke to your sister Agnes, do you remember Agnes?"

Peter continued to ramble on without pause, trapped in a frustration loop that had plagued many entrepreneurs throughout history - to have conceived a solution well ahead of the technology needed to implement it. Helen sat back and turned to Hickling for help, who lifted both hands in easy acceptance.

"You see what I mean."

Helen nodded.

James had been standing to one side, listening to Peter. He hesitated at first, but then, as if witnessing a struggling student, he felt compelled to help. "You need to abandon the ten-state system."

Peter's head turned to settle on James, and all fidgeting stopped. "Why? Why would you say that young man?"

James was taken aback, but Helen signaled for him to continue.

"For two reasons..."

"Namely?"

James picked up the pace. "Circuit simplicity and accuracy."

"What do you suggest?"

"Two-state, binary, using your relays for gate logic."

"Fascinating... how would you interface?"

"Key-code generator at the input, R/2R ladder at the output."

Helen sat back and waited as this conversation continued for quite some time, all the while watching Peter's anxiety dissipate as each of his problems were solved in turn. In a break, she whispered under her breath, "How did you do that, James?"

"I have a sixty-year history advantage."

Handing him the black book, Helem said, "Please, James."

"Peter, would you look at this for me?"

"Of course, young fella, anything... you know, you're a very clever chap. Cleverer than you look!" he said with a smile. "I believe you'll go far."

"Thank you. That's a great compliment coming from you."

Peter studied the contents, flitting through the pages. "Yes, yes, an early version of the enigma code. Four-wheel, four-letter offset... I believe it's in German." He sighed heavily, rubbing his eyes and yawning. "Do you mind if I take a short nap? I have depleted myself." His head drooped, though he recovered a little, and, before nodding off completely, he said, "Thank you, young man. You know, these breakthroughs are so bloody exhausting."

Chapter 5

The limousine traveled six kilometers from Zurich to the Savant Foundation estate. After crossing a bridge spanning the Limmat river, it passed through large wrought iron gates in the southwest corner of the grounds, waved on by security in the gatehouse. The paved driveway was flanked by chestnut trees while a parallel path for walkers cut through an avenue of lime trees. The manor had the country house characteristics of the Bernese nobility, and the park-like grounds were surrounded by hills and forested slopes, with the Alps as a backdrop.

The limousine pulled up to the front entrance, the driver exited smartly, and held open the passenger door. A mother, father, and young boy of around twelve years of age were escorted into the foyer. The child made loud smacking noises and when his arms got loose from his mother's iron grip, they would flail in the air as if controlled by a puppeteer. The main door led into a long corridor with several reception rooms to the left and right, finely furnished in the empire style with extensive art collections adorning the walls.

The parents hesitated, feeling out of place in such finery, but their escort encouraged them on. The corridor opened into a hexagonal hall in the center of the house, with staircases on opposite sides leading up to the second floor. They were shown into an elegant anteroom with displays showing carved and gilded altarpieces, costumes, dollhouses, medieval weaponry, and antique porcelain stoves, and, after knocking, a voice answered and they were shown into an expansive office.

A kindly, gray-haired, elderly gentleman was sitting at a large comfortable desk. He had a magnifying eyepiece and a set of intricate tools laid out and was calibrating the mechanism of an antique Swiss timepiece. On seeing the family, he removed the eyepiece, smiled warmly, and came quickly around the table, extending his hands in welcome.

"Mr. and Mrs. Timoshenko, my name is Hans Langsdorf, I am the director of the Savant Foundation, please take a seat."

The family looked at the ornate sofa, hesitated, and by way of a solution, the father removed a large handkerchief, laid it out carefully, and offered the spot to his wife.

Hans shook his head and clasped his hands in supplication.

"My dear sir, madam, there is no need for that, make yourselves comfortable. I am hoping you will come to consider this institute a home from home. Thank you for the consideration, but there is no need."

Hans pressed a button on his desk and in response, a lady entered, and Hans asked, "Can I offer you some refreshment? Coffee?"

"That would be very nice, thank you, sir."

"It is Hans, please." He pulled a chair close to seat himself opposite their son. "And this must be Semyon."

The boy rocked rhythmically in spite of his parent's restraint. Hans removed a spongy, spiked ball from his pocket and presented it to Semyon. With a squeeze, it glowed different colors and vibrated in response to different pressure points.

Semyon stopped moving, entranced, took the ball, and began to examine it with quiet, undivided attention. The parents showed visible relief in response, and Hans' assistant reentered to set out coffee and some small pastries.

Hans looked between them. "Is the hotel to your liking?"

The mother responded, "Very much so, sir... I'm sorry, Hans."

"And your journey?"

"Without incident, thank you."

"I hope our agent in Helsinki was attentive to all your needs?"

Mr. Timoshenko answered, "Yes, she was very kind, couldn't have been kinder... if I could speak plainly?"

"Please."

"We have only very modest means..." his wife dropped her head, "... we would sacrifice anything for him, but..."

Hans reached out and took them both by the hand. "Let me stop you there, my good man. We ask nothing of you, other than your faith in us to do the best for your son. You are doing us a great service, and for that I personally thank you. Our facility is staffed with the best pediatric neurologists, child psychiatrists, molecular geneticists, and, speech and occupational therapists. All committed to helping your son, and searching for the answers to autism."

The parents looked to Hans and then their son, and then through tears, the mother asked, "But why... why would you do all this for us?"

"I had an autistic son, years ago, Lukas, who I was unable to help at that time... it is my way of making amends... I recognize the hardship of being parted, and so I have instructed our agent to pay you a yearly stipend to enable you and your dear wife to come and visit Semyon whenever you wish." He removed a handkerchief with his embroidered initials from his pocket and passed it to Mrs. Timeshenko. "Please, my dear lady, I hate to see you cry."

Taking the handkerchief and wiping away tears, she said, "Thank you, sir… you don't know how much this means to us."

"Please, my good woman, it is I who should be thanking you… and you must call me Hans. Come now, we shall have our coffee, and then you must let me take you on a tour."

***

Like many of the high-end historic hotels in downtown Los Angeles, it had been built in the 1920s and had hosted the Oscars during the golden age of Hollywood. It had a mixture of Spanish beaux art styles with intricately painted wooden-beamed ceilings, travertine and oak paneled walls, bronze stairwells and doorways, hand-embroidered tapestries, and marble fountains. It took your breath away, and the young man entering the lobby stood for quite some time and just stared.

Seeing his ripped jeans and oversized, grungy T-shirt, the doorman made a beeline for him and asked, "Can I help you, sir?" He spoke these words with a tone that said, 'you don't belong here, turn and leave.'

"I'm here to see a Mr. Drummond?"

The doorman's demeanor changed entirely to one of deference. "This way sir." Taking him to a lounge just off the main lobby, he pointed to a well-dressed, distinguished-looking man of around fifty, reading a newspaper and having coffee.

"Mr. Drummond?"

"Yes, Jason?"

"Yes sir. I got your message and came straight from class. I'm sorry, I didn't have a chance to change. I look a bit of a mess."

"That's okay, please take a seat." He beckoned to the waiter nearby, and turned back to Jason. "Would you like something?"

"Coke, please. Thank you."

"You filled out an application for a scholarship in high school in Columbus, and attended two interviews."

Jason looked confused. "For the Hive Foundation? Yes, but nothing came of it."

"On the contrary, you passed."

Again, Jason looked puzzled.

"We needed to be sure your near-perfect GPA was not a flash in the pan. In this last year at Cal Poly, you have excelled in spite of all the obstacles."

He smiled appreciatively. "Thank you, sir."

"You drive a pick-up that will not pass smog, you wait tables for minimum wage plus tips, and live in a rented house with seven roommates. Hardly a conducive atmosphere for advancement."

"No."

"Well, we'd like to help."

"Great, thank you. Any help would be really appreciated."

"Our monthly remuneration will enable you to rent a very nice apartment on your own and give up your job, so you can direct all your attention to your studies."

"Really, wow! This is great… I could take more classes and finish sooner!"

"That sort of attitude…" he pointed directly at him, " is why we have chosen you. But we do have two conditions."

Quite unable to contain himself, he blurted out, "Anything!"

"Listen carefully, because this must be understood. Firstly, we wish to remain anonymous - tell anyone about us and our assistance ends. Secondly, we operate on a quid-pro-quo system. We do something for you and then we expect you to do something for us."

"Fair enough…" he laughed, "… as long as you don't want me to kill somebody!"

"Of course not… but we do expect absolute compliance when we want something in return - do you agree to our terms?"

"Yes, sir, I do."

Drummond smiled happily. "Now for the fun part. What car would you like?"

Jason held his breath, hoping this was not a joke. "Can I have anything?"

"Name it and I'll tell you."

"Mustang Shelby?"

"Nice choice… done!" He extended his hand. "Welcome to the Collective."

Chapter 6

It was Sunday evening, and James and Helen had the aunts over for dinner. The day still held some warmth so the French doors in the dining room were open, and dusk created an end-of-the-day peace, as shadows gathered and slowly grew as the sunset. Maria bustled in the kitchen, preparing coffee and dessert, with empty meat and vegetable platters and other dishes bearing witness to a successful meal.

The large dining table dominated the room but the occupants were grouped intimately in a corner. An aesthetical rather than functional fire burned in a brick fireplace to ward off the inevitable onshore marine layer, and this hearth had a thick oak beam mantle over which hung an antique mirror reflecting the companionable scene.

Leaning back in her seat, Helen called out, "Maria, please come and sit with us."

"No, no, I finishing now. I fine 'elen."

Aunt Rose asked, "So how did it go with Peter?"

Helen answered, "He and James hit it off! He was so helpful."

James continued, "They overcame such hurdles... what a talented group."

"I remember at Alan Turing's funeral, one of his colleagues said, he may not have won the war, but I dare say, we would have lost it without him... they treated that poor man so shabbily, considering."

James nodded. "Yes, so mean-spirited. I downloaded an enigma code simulator off the internet, set the offset Peter gave us, and ran the decoded text through a German translator."

Helen picked up the pocketbook. "He was such a nasty man. James took this from his pocket after he had died in the accident."

James took her hand in comfort. "Most of it was irrelevant details, but toward, the end it talks about the threat Helen and I created. He enacted an emergency protocol in this *cooperative group* of theirs, that gave him direct access to a man in London who was researching a more detailed profile on me." Looking directly at Helen, he added, "They could not fathom how we could have had such an edge, and known as much as we did."

Helen and Aunt Rose both answered in unison, "The Mind Link."

James nodded.

Maria was about to enter the dining room with a tray through a swinging door, but stopped and waited, listening intently.

Aunt May had been preoccupied with her food, indulging in the luxury of having someone other than herself cook, but this piqued her interest. "Mind Link?"

James dismissed this out of hand. "It's nothing, Aunt May."

May frowned, looking between James and Rose. "You know, Helen, whenever it was anything practical, James came directly to me, knowing full well my dear sister would be completely useless." Rose's eyebrows lifted in amusement. "Everything else, however, was her purview, as they both assumed I could not understand… Now, Helen, what are they talking about?"

A look of disapproval crossed James' face, and he interrupted. "How did your runner beans come in this year, Aunt May?"

"Very well, James, in fact…" May paused, realizing she'd

been intentionally derailed. "Oh no, you don't, young man," she waggled a finger in admonishment, "please continue, Helen."

Reluctantly she did. "Your very talented nephew developed a system that lets you relive your past in explicit detail."

"Well, I never, on a television?"

"No, in your mind's eye."

"Oh my."

"It's an odd experience. To revisit people and places from your past and see it all again, but in this case through an adult eye."

"So, you've tried this, Helen?"

"Yes."

"And I know you have, Rose?"

"Yes."

Turning to James, she said, "Then why haven't I?"

Helen jumped to his defense. "It caused nothing but trouble, Aunt May, and in the wrong hands, it could be very dangerous."

Maria entered the dining room with a tray of coffee press pots, cups, milk, sugar, and biscuits.

"Then why did you make this contraption in the first place, James?"

"To play back memories of Dad - I never expected it to work as well as it did."

Rose recalled her experience with the mind link. "Seeing lost loved ones again, it was… indescribable."

Aunt May was still confused. "But I don't understand."

Helen leaned in. "It lets you travel back in time and pull out any memory you want from deep in your subconscious mind and then play it back in your conscious mind. But it's so vivid, you feel the emotions of the time, sense the sun on your face, hear the bees, and smell the lavender."

"I see."

They all looked quizzically, trying to assess her degree of comprehension. May's eyes had turned inward.

Rose asked, "So, May dear if you could relive any moment in your life, what would it be?"

"The High Chaparral."

They all smiled, patiently realizing she hadn't grasped the concept.

But she continued, "It was broadcasted a little late every Thursday evening. That sweet little boy who had come to live with us would settle himself on the floor with his cowboy rifle, and I would watch him shoot the baddies, and hope we could make up for what he'd lost. Rose would paint and I would knit, and I realized then… this was happiness. I was part of a family, and it was the best time of my life."

Chapter 7

The drone of the engines and the low light level had lulled most of the first-class passengers to sleep, but Hannah sat glued to her laptop screen, working. She was wearing retro-style, pin-striped gray-blue pants, and a bleach white button-up dress shirt.

Marianne was seated next to her, eyes closed, earbuds in, listening to music. As she opened her eyes, a middle-aged businessman looked quickly away in an attempt to conceal his lustful gaze. Releasing her seatbelt, she stood up to wriggle her low-rise, ripped jeans up as they had slid down to an almost exposing level. Stretching provocatively, she pulled down her pink midriff top, exposing the soft curves of her full breasts, and opened the overhead bin, pretending to search for something. A sideways glance confirmed she had the full attention of the businessman, and almost every other awake passenger. She flopped back in her seat with a look of teenaged boredom.

Without looking up from the screen, Hannah tutted several times. "Marianne, behave."

"Yes, Hannah."

"Stay focused. We are on an emergency assignment."

With a mischievous smile, she said, "But it's so easy."

***

James felt that nagging sensation that something was wrong. He had assigned it several times to a past association with the little black book, but it didn't answer. He knew, all too well, that he had avoided resuming his career as this primeval instinct kept warning him to keep his head down. He dismissed it daily, but there it was again, and as with science, where he had learned to listen to the signs and had in fact achieved key breakthroughs when he tuned into this sense to uncover the slightest of nuance, as all had to be identified to fully comprehend all the parameters at play, and then determine which of these parameters were dominant.

He decided to jog, as exercise may not alleviate the root of the problem, but it would treat the symptoms. James came bounding down the stairs and was heading to Helen in the sitting room but changed direction due to the heavenly aroma coming from the kitchen. Seeing freshly-baked hot cross buns on a cooling rack, he playfully nabbed one as Maria's back was turned. She snapped uncharacteristically, but then tried, unsuccessfully, to soften her tone. "I wish you would ask first."

James replaced it, taken aback, "I'm sorry, Maria, that was silly of me."

Not looking up, she said, "Is okay, does not matter, take it now."

James left the kitchen, unable now to fully enjoy his ill-gotten gains. Walking into the living room, he found Helen and Rose sitting and talking. He leaned down to kiss each in turn.

Under his breath to Helen, he said, "What's the matter with Maria?"

"I'm not sure, but there's something. She won't tell me."

Purposefully, he posed a framed question to both of them. "Do you want me to come to town with you?"

Aunt Rose answered, without missing a beat. "Absolutely not."

Helen sealed it with, "You'll only be in the way."

With a farewell wave, he said, "Not wanted, I see! I'll go running then."

As he collected his phone from the hall stand and opened the front door, he hesitated and returned to lean back into the room.

"Take care of yourself, Helen."

A message passed between them, as they both smiled, and Rose looked on questioningly. Helen answered quickly to cover, "Of course, I will, silly."

Leaving again, James gave a sideways glance in the direction of the kitchen and stopped. "Do you want me to pick up anything, Maria, as I pass the village?"

There was a delay, and her voice broke a little. "No, thank you, Mr. James."

He was about to go to her to see if he could help alleviate what ailed her but heard her phone ring so decided against it and left, hitting the gravel of the driveway, running.

Helen and Rose collected their things and prepared to leave.

Rose's interest was piqued. "Is everything okay, Helen?"

"Yes, of course."

Rose was not easily deceived. "You are a little harder for me to read, but he's a dead giveaway."

As James jogged along the desolate and treacherous cliffs, Marianne was seen walking toward him on a perpendicular path. She had her cell phone to her ear, and a black SUV was parked a little way off. She was dressed up to the minute, as usual, in a tight, pale pink mini skirt, white sweater, and high, shiny black boots - totally incongruous for a country walk. "Wait… wait… wait …"

Meanwhile, Helen and Rose left the house and, reaching for her phone, Helen stopped for a moment, before realizing, "Oh dear, James has taken my phone by accident."

James had settled into a comfortable rhythm, his mind still grappling with a problem where he didn't know the question, let alone the answer.

Returning to the front door, Helen called out a message to Maria and then rejoined Rose: "Maria, in case he doesn't realize, can you tell James, he has taken my phone by accident, and I have his."

Maria dropped a dish, and after a moment's hesitation, she ran to Helen, her eyes wide in panic.

James converged on Marianne, still on her phone. "Wait… wait… now.'

James' phone rang at almost exactly the same time as Helen's. Lifting it to view the caller ID, he saw it was Aunt May.

Helen did the same, while her caller ID showed it to be her office. "Excuse me, Aunt Rose while I check this."

With a wave, Rose signaled to go right ahead.

Helen pressed the answer button and was lifting the handset when Maria came tearing out of the front door, startling them both, screaming, "DON'T ANSWER THAT!"

What saved Helen from the brunt of the sound spike was that she had only lifted the handset halfway to her ear, but it was still heard clearly, causing her head to drop back, her eyes and mouth to open, and her body to collapse in a slump. Rose's reflexes were fast enough to break her fall but as a consequence, she too lost her balance and fell.

Maria and Rose stared at each other, frozen, breathing short and shallow. Rose's eyes narrowed with distrust and disgust.

Maria composed herself, quickly accepting that the deceit had been fully realized and removed her apron, folding it carefully and placing it neatly at the entrance. She smoothed back her hair pulling herself up to her full height with a composure that was not there before.

"I was concerned…" she smiled at the irony of this statement with sadness, "…it was only a brief pulse, but…".

The broken English was replaced by a clean American accent with an air of deliberate exactness. Looking down at Helen, she was relieved to see her murmur and move.

"Some people have reacted badly, and it has caused… could you please explain. She will not understand, but very few options were open to me." Hesitating for a moment, she turned, walked to her car, climbed in, and drove away.

James answered his call. "Yes, Aunt May, No it's me, James. I must have taken Helen's phone by mistake." James glided past Marianne at a fast pace, leaving her quickly behind.

Marianne turned her head from him, dumbstruck, and when he had passed, she slammed her cell phone against a nearby rock in frustration and threw it out to sea in a blind rage.

Chapter 8

From the bluff that overhung James and Helen's home, an ambulance could be seen leaving, but a police car remained. The two officers had taken statements from everyone and were now in their vehicle radioing in their status and completing their report.

Although the paramedics had strongly recommended Helen go to the hospital for testing and observation, she had refused.

James came out of the house with backpacks and a shoulder bag which he loaded into the backseat of his car. Helen was seated with Rose under a shady garden alcove with climbing plants trained over a latticed wooden framework. As he approached, he overheard Aunt Rose. "If it's any conciliation, Helen dear, she did say to tell you she had very little choice."

"But Maria… I just can't believe it."

James put his hand on her shoulder, "I know this is a great shock, but…"

"I know, this is not the time."

Taking Helen's hand, she said, "I'm sorry love." Turning to Rose, she added, "Aunt May is packing for you both.

"Do you really think this is necessary?"

Helen stood. "Yes, you must… please, Aunt Rose."

"Okay dear, better safe than sorry, I suppose."

James stared at Rose, "As far as where to go, you and I know the best place for you and Aunt May… without saying it, I mean."

Helen was confused. "Why, without saying it?"

"I understand," said Rose, comprehending. "Maria will have told them about the Mind Link."

"And if they get access to it, and me, they'll find the two of you. These people are thorough, Aunt Rose."

"I see... and yes, James, I do know where would be best."

Handing her a note, he said, "When you're settled, order this service to call me using a pc. It's called VOIP. It can't be traced."

Placing the note in her pocket, Rose took Helen in her arms. "No long goodbyes now. You are stronger than you know, Helen, you must tap into that strength, especially now."

Helen kissed and hugged her. "Please look after yourselves, I couldn't bear it if anything happened to either of you."

Looking at the two of them, she smiled confidently, pausing a while to register the moment.

"May and I have weathered adversity before." Patting them both affectionately on the cheek, then sternly to James, she said, "If this is as bad as you say, do not hesitate to do whatever is necessary, do you hear me James... and in circumstances such as these, you must think rather than feel." Squeezing both their hands, she smiled again lovingly, turned quickly, and left.

***

The SUV rolled over the rocky terrain to pick up Marianne, who walked briskly toward it and climbed in the back to take her seat alongside Hannah who had her laptop open with a wireless headset. Covering the mouthpiece, she said, "I couldn't reach you... reception problems?"

Marianne had calmed a little. "Yes. What went wrong?"

Covering the mouthpiece again, she said, "Phone mix-up. They sound-spiked his wife, I'm waiting for an update." She lifted a hand to signal a communication coming in and for Marianne to wait. "Yes, I understand. Yes, I agree." Touching the headset to end the call, she covered the mouthpiece and tapped the driver's shoulder. "Moore's home."

Marianne smiled in anticipation, "Is the order still to acquire?"

"Yes," and then into her open communication channel, she asked, "Are they still there?"

Chapter 9

May came lumbering down the stairs carrying two huge suitcases. Rose looked on, flabbergasted. "May, dear, I said essentials. We will buy new when we are settled."

"Rose, I'm leaving half my wardrobe as it is. Surely you wouldn't begrudge me my undergarments and night attire?"

"One set of each in an overnight bag, and one change of clothes."

"And what of toiletries?"

Rose was alerted when the sun's reflection from a windshield swiped across the living room wall. Moving closer to the window, she parted the net curtains. "We must leave now, May. Go as quickly as you can, I'll be right behind you."

The two operatives watched the house and saw the curtains twitch. "There's movement from inside, they haven't attempted to leave, ma'am."

Hannah's voice could be heard. "Move in. Kill both, but make it look like a robbery gone wrong."

The two operatives exited quickly. One went straight to the front door and kneeled, the other to the rear of the house. When at the back door he reported, "In position," and in response the other said, "Go." They simultaneously elbowed out a small window pane in the doors, reached in to release the latches, and moved inside, removing slender switchblades and having them at the ready.

***

Hannah's SUV reached the driveway leading to James and Helen's house and stopped. She studied the lay of the land, seeing the two police officers, no sign of James and Helen but their car door was open.

A voice came over the open channel from the lead operative at the aunt's home. "They appear to have barricaded themselves into a living room. We're forcing our way in now."

"Get it done," said Hannah, her focus now on what was in front of her.

Marianne leaned forward keenly. "Let me, Hannah?"

Hannah ignored her and gave an order to the driver. "Block the exit and draw the police to us, away from their car."

Marianne moved closer to Hannah, sliding her hand slowly across her leg, and then teasingly to her inner thigh. "Let me, Hannah, please."

The two police officers looked on confused as the SUV blocked the driveway, and the driver gestured for them to come with an impatient wave. Not recognizing the SUV or the driver, they looked on, confused, and annoyance took over at them being summoned so disrespectfully. With a look and nod of agreement, they strode towards the SUV.

Marianne kissed Hannah's neck as she continued to caress and press rhythmically with her hand.

Hannah watched the approaching officers through the windshield, and her driver turned his head slightly, indicating a growing concern for instructions. Hannah's face lost composure as she relaxed and her eyes closed in pleasure. Snapping out of it, she curbed her emotions.

"Okay, but quickly, Marianne, this is not our objective.

Driver, do nothing."

Marianne pulled away excitedly, slid off the seat, slipped out through the door on the blind side, crouched down, and quietly clicked the door closed. The officers arrived and signaled for the driver to lower his window. He remained motionless, staring straight ahead, his hands resting on the wheel.

Peering through the glass into the back seat, the second officer could see Hannah, who was on a call, saying, "What do you mean? They are two old ladies. Explain."

A faint but clear reply could be heard. "They're gone. Not a sign of them. They've disappeared!"

The officer tapped the window. "Lower the window, ma'am."

Hannah ignored him and raised her voice in irritation to the operative. "Do you realize how ridiculous you sound? Find them."

Marianne peered under the SUV at the feet of the officers. Having no luck with Hannah, the officer continued circling the car. Seeing this, Marianne got to her feet but crouched below the window line and moved like a cat around to the back of the vehicle. Her hand grasped the M-shaped buckle of her belt, her forefingers sliding neatly into the two arches of the handle. She slowly pulled out a concealed custom tri-blade which attached to her hand as naturally as a prosthetic implant.

Stepping away from the vehicle, she straightened to her full height, placed her weapon hand behind her back, and brushed off her outfit with particular care. Approaching the officer with her best smile, he looked her up and down appreciatively and responded to her with pleasure. Hannah watched through the window as Marianne raised her tri-blade and struck with such speed, bringing it down violently and at a deliberate angle to enter the officer's neck, simultaneously severing his jugular vein and piercing his voice box. Without missing a beat, Marianne stepped over his collapsed and writhing body as he clasped his throat, blood spewing through his fingers and from his open gasping mouth and nose.

James caught this coup-de-grace through an upstairs window. "Helen, we have to leave now!"

Marianne quickened her pace toward the other officer still attempting to give orders to the motionless driver. Concealing her weapon behind her back once again, she feinted a stumble and reached out her free hand to him for assistance. He obliged willingly, and as he looked down to ascertain the cause of her trouble, he missed the tri-blade entering his neck with such violence. Grimacing in pain, he searched her face for an answer as to why, before dropping to his knees and falling face-down into the dirt.

For the first time, Marianne appeared troubled as she twisted and turned to check her outfit for any blemishes. Placing a foot on the now motionless body, she pulled at his shirt, loosened a section, and meticulously cleaned her blade. When she was satisfied, she returned it to its sheath, and skipped around the car, opened the door, and took her seat.

Chapter 10

It was a pretty day, neither warm nor cold, and the sun came out from behind the clouds intermittently to light up the church of St. Clements. Like many of its type, it had been built sometime after the Norman conquest in 1066, and had been added to and altered over the next several hundred years, with a major reconstruction in the 1300s. It was made using coursed limestone rubble, had a square tower, and an attached rectangular nave or main section. The paired belfry windows, embattled parapets, pinnacles, and gargoyles gave it a classic gothic appearance.

The wedding guests arrived in dribs and drabs, dressed to the nines, and were shown to their seats by ushers observing all the rules of convention. The groom and best man took their position early, the vicar entered in bright robes checking to see all was ready before taking his place and, in so doing, triggered the bride and her father to walk down the aisle and join the group at the altar.

After a suitable pause to mark this auspicious occasion, the vicar began. "Welcome..." Three knocks were heard near the pulpit. He ignored this and carried on, "Dearly beloved, we are..."

"Hello... Hello!" Now, this was clear but distant, giving it an eerie tone which conjured up thoughts of haunted churches. "Is anyone there?"

The father of the bride took the initiative. "We hear you."

"Good. There is a latch near the lectern that ingeniously

blends in with the tiled floor. Can you release it, please?"

A small deputation was now searching fruitlessly for this latch that had been cleverly engineered during the early 1500s to be unseen until the vicar came to their rescue and pointed it out. Releasing the catch and opening the trap door, a flashlight could be seen down a set of ancient stone steps leading into a cavern which looked as though it went into the bowels of the earth. Two elderly voices could be heard bickering, and then out walked Rose and May in their hats and coats, each carrying an overnight bag.

The vicar was incredulous but recognized them immediately. "What in heaven's name are the two of you up to?"

All at once realizing they had stepped into, and severely disrupted, a ceremony, they tried to make suitable signs of apology which were wholly inadequate considering, as they hastened their retreat. Passing the front pews of gawping immediate family members, Aunt May felt compelled to offer up some sort of explanation. "It's an old priest hole… for catholic priests, during the Reformation."

The bride's mother was appalled. "What? I am not having my daughter married in a Catholic church!"

The groom's mother retaliated immediately, and just as loudly from across the aisle. "This is high C of E, what's wrong with that stupid woman?"

Rose and May left an escalating squabble behind them as they picked up their pace and, not slowing down but with a slight inclination of her head, Rose said, "It would have been better to leave things well alone, May dear."

***

James drove the car off the path and cut directly across a field, passing thoroughly disinterested cows. The frame bounced and shook, and the suspension creaked with the strain. Helen held on tight while watching, out of the rear window, the pursuing vehicle. Leaving the field through a narrow gate, James could see the metal rolling cattle rails, so he slowed and made sure he drove straight across the bars before turning sharply and speeding off down a small, winding country lane.

Hannah and Marianne didn't fare so well. Their driver hit the bars fast and at an angle, slipping, skidding, and slamming hard with a jarring thud into a walled bank. The embarrassed driver tried to recover as quickly as he could but they had lost a lot of ground, and Hannah and Marianne looked on as James and Helen's car turned a corner and was gone. Hannah brought up a local map on her laptop, and, into her still-open communication channel with the other operatives, she snapped, "Forget the aunts. Head toward the A39, I will update you."

Helen looked again to reassure herself they were gone, and James allowed himself a quick glance in the rearview mirror - they had lost them for now. It was a fleeting victory, though, as his eyes registered their reappearance, making up the loss with reckless abandon.

The next turn showed a line of milking cows crossing the narrow country lane from pasture to milking sheds. Traveling at breakneck speed, James slammed on the brakes, and gray plumes of burning rubber rose from the corners of the car and it skewed slightly before coming to a stop. The farmer came running, waving his crook in anger, and as the spooked cows in the car's path pulled away to create an opening, James slipped through the gap. The SUV was now right behind them and capitalized on the opportunity to weave its way through the same gap without delay.

Marianne slapped the driver on the shoulder. "Watch the cows! Do not hit the cows!" She clumped him again. "Are you listening to me?"

"Yes, miss," he replied irritably, his mind taken up completely with the job at hand.

Hannah intervened. "He will be careful, Marianne, now let him do his job." To the driver, she said, "I am guessing he will turn right at the next junction," and then into her open channel, "Go south on the B3237."

Watching James' car, they were all relieved when Hannah's prediction came true, and, as he made the turn sharply and accelerated away, Hannah spoke to her second car.

"He's coming right to you, block him," and then, tapping the driver's shoulder, she added, "Pull back slightly and when he hesitates on seeing our other car, fishtail him."

The two cars sped down the lane as if they were attached and at crests, both cars were momentarily airborne. A view opened up to show the approaching village and Helen took hold of James' arm as they both realized and spoke in unison, "It's market day."

The single-lane Roman bridge connected the two halves of the ancient village of Treacombe. It was densely packed with livestock and locals crossing to and fro, but congregated in a large open field filled with pens, tractors, and stalls selling all manner of produce and crafts. The two operatives who had been called upon to set up a roadblock were trapped on the other side of the bridge, unable to convince anyone to allow them to pass.

James did not slow down his car. If anything, he appeared to speed up toward the impassable bridge off in the distance.

"We will have to leave the car, Helen."

Veering off down a side street and squeezing between two buildings which appeared too tight to allow his car to pass, he pulled into a wooded enclave, leaped from the car while gathering up their bags, and they took off on foot through a clump of trees to an open, empty field.

The SUV driver followed James more cautiously through the gap between the buildings, not used to the smaller roads of England. Hannah watched James and Helen emerge from the thicket and messaged the other operatives to converge on their position.

On reaching a ridge, James and Helen paused to look back at two men and two women following at a steady but slower pace.

In the field beyond the ridge was a disused brick engine house and crumbling tin mine stack, and beyond that, railroad tracks that crossed their path and entered a train station near the coast. To the right, a deep estuary ran under the train tracks, banked by hillocky sand dunes, and finally to the sea with large rollers pounding the line of sand.

Helen was catching her breath. "Don't we need to go? Do you know what you're doing, James?"

James checked the time on his phone, looked up, and smiled at Helen, taking her hand. "Don't worry, Helen… this is my backyard."

Chapter 11

Hannah, Marianne, and their two operatives were moving along at a slow jogging walk, with Hannah bringing up the rear. They had left the driver with the SUV awaiting instructions and walked down a rutted lane which had led them up to this high field bordered by ancient stone walls. The land up here was rockier with clusters of whale-shaped grey boulders wearing coats of dark green lichen. Overhead, they heard the screeching calls of seagulls flying inland, accompanying a marine layer coming in with the tide. James and Helen had stopped on the ridge line, and Hannah deduced they must be in some sort of trouble or had no escape path.

On their pursuing trek, the group had now been joined by two excited border collies, who dropped to the ground in a playful herding stance. As they climbed, Hannah was afforded a better view and called the driver, "Go back about half a mile, there is a gate that will lead to us – you should be able to handle the terrain."

Marianne was beside herself with joy. "Look at them, Hannah! Look at them! Come here, my babies."

Hannah spoke to the operatives, "Go ahead as quickly as you can, acquire only."

"Yes, ma'am, acquire only."

Sprinting away, the operatives appeared to have activated the dogs' inherent instinct to contain the group and they raced after them, first barking, then blocking, and finally nipping at their ankles, bringing one of them down. In a rapid, conditioned response, he pulled out his gun and shot the dog dead, holstered his gun, and was about to carry on, when he heard an inhuman wild scream.

Marianne went straight at him, a woman possessed, and in a lightning-fast move she extracted her tri-blade, swinging at his face with several wild but expert backhand and forehand swipes. If he hadn't had training in hand-to-hand combat, this melee would have cut him to ribbons, but even still, she always had him on the defensive, ducking, pulling back, and always giving ground. Tripping backward, he fell and Marianne leaped at a height that would put a leopard to shame, pulling back her tri-blade in mid-flight, landed on all fours on his chest, and was about to deliver her finishing blow when she was kicked off the man by Hannah, with all her might, shouting, "Eliver , arrêtez, vous chienne stupide."

Marianne showed no sign of recognizing Hannah and assumed an attack position, the tri-blade pulled back ready to lunge, her hands shaking with rage, eyes on fire, and breathing hard through gritted teeth.

"Marianne, nous avons un travail de faire."

Marianne turned her head reluctantly, stamped her feet and pulled away, dropped to her knees, and swooped up the dead dog into her arms, pulling it close to her in an embrace which smeared blood over her white sweater.

Hannah offered her hand to the stunned operative, pulled him to his feet, and waved him away. "Leave us, I will stay with her. Get them."

The two operatives left as Marianne screamed, rocking back and forth with the dog in her arms. "Vous hybride! Hybride!"

Chapter 12

On leaving the church, Rose and May left the high street and took Church Hill down to the Old Town of St. Clements. The streets here were cobbled, the old shops were rickety and the unbelievably quaint cottages had wonky walls with immaculately kept, small front gardens. Continuing on, they reached the brown clapboard fisherman huts which were all open as the tide had brought in all of the brightly-colored fishing boats and they were in the process of unloading their catch. There was the click and clack of the boats' bobbing masts, the indecipherable calls of the fisherman, and the insistent screeching of the seagulls as they waited impatiently for scraps, but they didn't notice these, as they were as they should be. St. Clements's families had been fishing this coast for generations and they called after them with warm greetings, and May was offered a choice cut of the fresh catch of the day, which she accepted and tucked into her handbag.

Rose saw what she was looking for and crossed over the small beach of cockle shells to a sea-going trawler with its engine running. A young man in slicker pants, Wellington boots, and a thick, brown wooly jumper came halfway across the plank and helped Rose and May aboard.

May kissed him on his cheeks. "We insist on paying, Jeremy."

"No, no, no, I wouldn't hear of it."

Rose took him by the arm. "Nonsense, we insist. This must put you out?"

"Not at all, I was going out tomorrow anyway." To his mate in the wheelhouse, he said, "Cast off, and take us out." Returning to Rose and May, he said, "And besides, if I took any money from you, my mum would tan me up, down, and sideways."

***

The black SUV bounced its way over the ridge and then down to the two operatives, still searching fruitlessly for James and Helen.

Hannah got out of the car, leaving Marianne subdued and non-verbal.

She approached the lead operative. "Well?"

"I don't understand, they can't get over the train tracks, there's a barbed wire fence."

"I'm getting sick of your incompetence. You will be on a charge for this."

"I'm sorry, ma'am, they just disappeared."

"That is the second time today you have used that word," and then, with annunciation, she said, "Never... say... disappeared... to me... again."

Hannah scanned the wide-open area. How did they do that?

Lifting her phone, she said, "I'm going to need two more units, now."

James and Helen made their way through a dank, dark abandoned tin mine tunnel, bent forward, with their phone's flashlights lighting the way. A loud rumble overhead alarmed Helen.

Checking the time, James said, "It's only a train, love. We are directly under the tracks now. But we must hurry to time this right."

"How did you know about this mine?"

"My friend and I discovered it and we would walk to and from school this way. Otherwise, it's a four-mile hike to a bridge to get across the tracks." There was light now, at the end of the passage, and they climbed up a steel ladder and under a barrier, which was signposted: keep to marked paths - previous mining area.

Hannah picked up James and Helen on the other side of the railroad tracks, running toward the station. Walking to the car, she reached in and grabbed a pair of binoculars. "I underestimated them."

James and Helen ducked under a fence, crossed the road, and headed to the entrance of the train station. The long, rectangular main building was in the French chateau style with Venetian gothic accents. It was situated in a dell and virtually on the beach, with a single road leading down from the town. The oversized roof had sweeping gables covered with layered patterns of slate, and an off-centered ornamental tower and open bay with Venetian columns marking the entrance. As they entered the ticket hall, the roof rafters gave the impression of a medieval hall, and opposite the ticket counter was a coffee bar, which Helen eyed immediately.

James knew her penchant for coffee. "We have time Helen, and can you grab something for us to eat on the train?"

As she crossed the foyer, Helen glanced out of the entrance to see their pursuers high on the hill. "Will do."

The ticket clerk on the other side of the small barred window was a shrewish little man whom James remembered from years past, and the recognition was apparently mutual. "Aren't you Rose and May's boy?"

"Yes. Good memory."

"You went off to America."

"That's right."

He shook his head in disapproval. "There was no need for that."

Helen joined him at the counter, and James took advantage of the situation. "This is my wife, Helen."

"Hi, nice to meet you." Her American accent was easily detected and he recoiled in disgust.

"I don't know what the world is coming to."

They both chuckled. Looking at the large hands of the Victorian clock, James knew that timing was critical. "Two for Hartland."

Helen was confused. "South, James?"

James gave her the 'can't explain now' look. "Yes Helen," and then to the clerk, he said, "The twelve past four, right?"

"Yes. Platform one... should be along shortly."

After going through the ticket check, they walked along the near-empty platform, sipping coffee, and Helen looked up again to see a flash from Hannah's binoculars. "They can see us, James."

"I'm counting on it."

"Why south? It dead-ends in two stops."

The southbound train rolled into the station.

"Peter and I would buy a cheap one-stop ticket south, and..." James' eyes glanced in the opposite direction to monitor a northbound train also coming to a stop on the opposite platform. They both came to an almost simultaneous stop.

Hanna watched them through her binoculars and could see James walk down the platform past several doors before they both climbed in. She lifted her phone.

"Send both units to the next southbound station and grab

them, the sixth carriage. Do whatever it takes."

Inside the carriage, the windows of the two trains were in perfect alignment, and Helen climbed through into the northbound train. After James had passed through their bags and coffees, he climbed through himself and they stayed far away from the opposite window.

Hannah ran to the car. "Finally, we have them!"

Chapter 13

The Savant Foundation sat nestled in its pastoral setting surrounded by rolling meadows blanketed in wildflowers. This gave way to dense alpine forests and then snow-capped mountain ranges. It was a storybook landscape in which the manor house and its accompanying buildings had a lost-in-time appearance.

Hans was in his office, watching an autistic boy and his aide on a monitor. The aide hovered over the boy, signaled what was wanted, and he cooperated by climbing into a recliner. He was mesmerized by the holographic projection over the armrest which showed a detailed depiction of the planets revolving around the solar flaring sun. The control booth director's voice could be heard faintly, although nobody else was in this sound-proofed hexagonal room.

"Output is in position... begin receptive conditioning sequence." A flat-screen attached to a robotic arm lifted up and took a position directly in front of him, and displayed a complex sheet of music. A second robotic arm presented an electronic keyboard, and the boy looked down and turned his eyes up to the screen at an awkward angle, and began to play an extremely complex piano sonata. A second picture within the frame showed the four isolated hive cells, with two of the four now occupied.

Hans' assistant walked in. "It's time, sir."

Hans walked into a luxurious auditorium, shadowed by his secretary. As he made his way to the podium, he was greeted by hearty applause and many shook his hand and he reciprocated, remembering each of the twenty-odd seated parents, who, with great affection, embraced and kissed him in the European style.

A sectioned and unobtrusive deputation of the international press was off to one side, taking pictures and shooting footage.

Taking the side stairs to the stage, he was handed a page by his secretary, and he placed it on the lectern. Behind him hung a banner that read: Savant Research Facility - a new way!

After a sweep to make eye contact with the room, he began.

"Thank you so much, all of you, for coming…" he nodded to the press, "I hope you don't mind the intrusion, but as you know, they have been very helpful in finding me all of you!"

Lifting a hand and clicking his fingers, a huge video screen came alive, showing a sweeping shot of the facility.

"We have put together a video tour to show you the great advances we are making in our new state-of-the-art savant research facility."

As Hans continued, a sweeping shot passed through the large, open double doors of the facility and into the research facility, which opened to a large, sky-lighted, open plan hexagon showing a central play area with swings, slides, and climbing apparatus. As the one-on-one supervised children play, we saw them walking on their toes, flapping their arms, throwing tantrums at being taken away, but always avoiding eye contact.

The lights had been dimmed but Hans continued. "Years ago, autistic-savant children were put into institutions and given a lobotomy, robbing the world of a precious treasure. When I first formed this foundation, the conventional wisdom of the day believed autism was caused by 'refrigerator mothers' who stunted their child's development by withholding affection. Later discredited, it was replaced by a theory that foods, additives, and then vaccinations triggered the child's affliction. Today, using advanced technology to study the brain's anatomy, and through consistent observation and empirical data, we believe we are close to discovering the root cause."

The video showed the research facility, as Hans continued his voice-over, and the shot circled the perimeter to show an occupational therapist helping a child with physical problems, a speech therapist working with communication disorders, child psychologists dealing with emotional problems, a brain neurologist studying a brain scan, a multi-sensory room filled with lights and textures, dining and sleeping quarters, and a pediatrician checking a child's abdomen.

"We have a gifted young lady who can draw horses in a renaissance perspective, a young man who can extract the mathematical root of a twelve-digit number in less than a second, and another young man who can read and memorize the left and right pages of a book simultaneously and can access any of the data in his nearly eight thousand repertoire in seconds. There are believed to be fewer than fifty autistic-savants alive in the world today. We have only nine here at this foundation. We have another young lady whose savant skill only emerged after her head was struck in a car accident, which suggests these skills reside in us all, and can possibly be unlocked."

The light level returned and Hans' secretary pointed subtly to her watch.

Hans took the hint. "Oh, oh, I'm going on too long, and a lovely lunch awaits us. But let me close by simply defining our differences. You and I take in every tiny detail through sight, sound, touch, taste, and smell... we process it, and edit out the most important information into a single useful idea that we then become conscious of. Our savant children cannot perceive the world with more than one sense at a time, and so they focus all their attention on one favored sensory channel. Another key difference is that the children are able to see the unconscious processing of the brain, making them innately aware of their sensed information to a fantastic detail."

Hans walked forward and bowed. "Thank you so much for coming."

The applause was almost deafening and did not stop. After a time, he signaled with his hands to stop and they did.

"Now, please join me and I look forward to speaking with each of you."

Chapter 14

As they gazed east, they could see the dome of St. Paul's Cathedral and James couldn't help but wonder what its architect, Wren, would make of the square mile of skyscrapers nearby.

Turning the corner they saw The Drovers Arms, and like so many of the London pubs, it was adorned with colorful hanging baskets up high, flower boxes at each window, and bedecked with so much ivy that the building's frontage could hardly be seen. James held the door open for Helen and they entered.

The signature smell engulfed their olfactory glands - a blend of hops, malt, spirits, and wet rugs from spilt ale. Whiskey jugs hung from the Tudor beams of the ceiling, portraits of English history crammed the walls, and a coal fire burned to ward off the nip in the air. It was lunchtime and so the stained-glass windows created a kaleidoscope of light which played on the solid wooden tables surrounding the bar. Cleverly placed partitions created little nooks and cubbies to accommodate groups of various sizes.

They had entered the private section and as they made for the bar, Helen smiled and pointed out an outmoded sign hanging above, which read, Only gentlemen will be served at this bar.

This section was filled with bankers, Fleet Street journalists, and the like, having their lunch and a pint, with their eyes glued to their phones.

The bartender approached. "Sir, madam, what can I get for you?"

"Scotch and American, two, please."

"Right you are."

Looking across the bar into the public section, Helen noticed it was packed and that they all wore red football jerseys. The jukebox was silent, as were the pinball machines, the dartboard was not in use and they were somber, almost morose.

On seeing her interest, the Barman whispered confidentially, "They're Manchester United fans, luv. Played Arsenal and lost badly. Waiting for their tour bus home."

Paying for the drinks, James' eye movement drew Helen's attention to a man sitting alone in an alcove, reading a book. With a fresh pint of bitter and a half-eaten ploughman's lunch in front of him, he was in his late forties, thinning black hair, dowdy in an accountant-like way, and he projected a despondent air.

They approached him and James asked, "Gregory Kerry?"

With a look of surprise, he said, "Yes?"

Outside the pub, a few patrons had come out to sit on benches or stand and enjoy the warmth of the day. Two heavily tinted sedans pulled up to the curb, the lead having Hannah, Marianne, and their usual driver inside them. Two operatives exited the other vehicle and came to Hannah's now open window. She put a finger to her earpiece to listen.

"As expected, they've made contact. You don't have firearms, right?"

They both nodded. "No, as you instructed ma'am."

"Good. When they leave, Mr. Moore will predictably hold open the door for his wife. Grab her, close the door on him until we have left. You will then start a fight with Mr. Moore to get you all arrested. Once contained, we can access our sources with the Metropolitan Police to pick him up. Are we clear?"

In unison, they replied, "Clear, ma'am."

James and Helen were met with cold indifference, but James

carried on regardless. "My name is James Moore, and this is my wife, Helen, and I wondered if you could help us?"

"I'm sure I couldn't," he replied and returned to his book.

"You haven't heard the question yet," snapped James irritably.

Kerry continued reading and didn't respond.

Helen took a seat opposite. "About three years ago, you were told to research my husband. We have a book that has all your contact information."

Closing his book, he looked at Helen indignantly, as she continued. "Could you just tell them, please, we made a mistake, we're sorry... could they just let it go?"

With a full laugh from a face that had no laugh lines, he shook his head incredulously. "It's too late... it's too late."

James grabbed him by the jacket in uncharacteristic frustration. "If you can't help us you bastard, just say so, but don't take such pleasure in being so unhelpful."

The barman called out sternly. "Oy, you two. I'll have none of that in 'ere!"

Releasing the unresponsive and still smirking Kerry, James and Helen looked around at the other patrons who pretended not to have noticed the altercation and decided it was time to leave.

Kerry called after them, "You woke the tiger, Mr. Moore, and it will have its pound of flesh."

On seeing them move toward the door through a side window, the two operatives moved quickly into position on either side of the door. As it opened, one snatched Helen's arm and yanked her out, while the second operative shouldered the door closed and jammed his foot at the base.

James was almost thrown off his feet by the slamming door.

Looking through the mullioned glass, he watched helplessly

as Helen was manhandled into the rear seat and sandwiched between Hannah and Marianne before being driven off at high speed. Trying the door again and finding it wouldn't budge, he put his shoulder to it several times with more and more aggression, but to no avail. Looking again through the glass, he saw the operative that had grabbed Helen, turn and walk back to join his accomplice with deliberate intent.

James' eyed the door and turned to see everyone watching him and the barman on the phone. As the panic for Helen's safety overwhelmed him, he arrested it as Rose's advice came into the forefront of his mind, loud and clear. Seeing a flip-down latch at the bottom of the door, he set it down with his foot just in time to resist a hefty shove from the other side and then slid the heavy locking bolts at the top and bottom of the door.

Unable to get in, even with their combined effort, the operatives looked through the glass to see James moving quickly through to the public section, and in response, they ran to that entrance. As James burst into the dismally silent room, the group turned in irritation at having their grief interrupted, and in his best Manchester accent, he shouted, "Two London wankers trying to kick me 'ead in. Said I was a Man U loser!"

The door opened and the operatives saw James standing motionless at the connecting door and moved toward him with aggression. The first was tripped up and got a Doc Martin boot full in the face as the second received a pint glass hard across the back of his head, and while they were both down, waves upon waves of red jerseys enveloped them.

Chapter 15

Weaving quickly around this brawl, James dashed out of the bar and looked to the end of the street as the sedan turned left, battling heavy traffic. Cutting the corner by running down a side road, he flew past street market stalls selling antiques and bric-a-brac to emerge just in time to see the car make a right toward Piccadilly Circus. He scanned up and down the street and ran into traffic, hailing a taxi, and climbed in.

"You're keen, mate," said the driver in a strong cockney accent.

"Follow that car," said James, and then realized how ludicrously cliche that sounded, so he added, "They have my wife."

The driver took off at speed, and his eyes met James' in the rearview mirror. They were kind eyes in a round, jovial face.

"I've waited all my life for a follow that car," he said with a laugh that shook his heavy-set, rotund frame.

James sat on the edge of his seat, taking off his shoulder bag and looking anxiously through the windshield as they battled traffic congestion to gain ground.

The cabbie caught his eyes again. "I can radio in for a bobby?"

With dread, he said, "No!"

"You fink they might knock 'er on the 'ead?"

James was about to explain, and then, for the sake of efficiency, opted to adopt his logic. "That's it, yes."

They had positioned themselves to within six cars now, and James pulled out his laptop, deep in thought. Getting even closer, he looked at the license plate.

"It's a seventy-one, right?"

"Right, two-fousand and twenny one."

James quickly searched 'keyless entry white papers.'.

"What're you doing, mate?"

"Trying to get the keyless entry code range and syntax variations for that car. What is it?'

"Merc, S430 sedan."

James scanned through to manufacturer, year, and model number. The next window called for a vin. He searched 'buy 2021 Mercedes S430.' The car dealers showed vin numbers, and he copied one into the keyless entry application window. A replacement unit was shown and when he clicked on 'tech. spec,' it described coding combinations and syntax range.

"They ain't gonna just give it out, are they?"

"No, but they will give me the range of possibilities, and then I can run a routine to generate every possible combination." Writing this routine and initiating the algorithm he looked up."

"How'll you know when you got it?"

"Watch," said James, pointing ahead. "I'm using only trunk codes right now."

They both watched patiently, and after a few moments, the trunk mysteriously popped open and flipped up. James stopped the routine.

The Mercedes pulled over, and Marianne got out, closed the trunk, returned, and the car pulled back into traffic.

"How would you like to make a thousand pounds?"

The cabbie smiled. "A grand? Cash?"

"Yes," said James, removing a wad of one hundred pound

notes from his pocket.

Laughing conspiratorially, he said, "The name's Nobby," as he offered his hand through the sliding glass window. "You're on, boss!"

"It's James... and the person we are trying to save is my wife, Helen." He handed him his laptop through the window and placed it alongside him. "When you press the T key, it will pop the trunk again."

"Boot?"

"That's right... do you want me to make it the B key?"

Laughing, he said, "Just having you on, Jimmy."

"I see," James replied, having no sense of humor at this time. "You will start this by pressing the T key. When I get my wife out and slam the door, press the L key, and the routine will repeatedly lock their doors at a very fast rate... have you got it?"

Lifting a thumb in acknowledgment, he said, "T fer trunk, L fer lock, on your word."

"Great, and thanks for this, Nobby."

The cab moved into a position behind the sedan, and the trunk popped open again. As the Mercedes pulled over and stopped, the cab followed suit, and James quickly exited the cab to meet Marianne, unnoticed from behind at the exact moment as when she leaned in to inspect the catch. James scooped her up and unceremoniously threw her into the trunk, just catching a glimpse of the shocked, indignant rage on her face before the lid slammed shut. Reaching into the car, he whisked Helen out, easily overcoming the unsuspecting Hannah who was talking on the phone but attempted a late lunging grab before the door was slammed in her face. The door latches could be heard clicking rapidly, and the car rocked as the frustrated driver and Hannah tried desperately to unlock and exit the car.

Helen and James climbed quickly into the cab, and it made a harrowing U-turn to the honks and shouts from cars and darted down an alley all while Nobby laughed and howled uncontrollably.

James and Helen embraced as the car's momentum forced them to slide from one end of the back seat to the other.

"Are you sure you're okay, Helen?"

"I'm fine, babe, nothing like a bit of excitement to get the adrenalin pumping!"

With tears of laughter spilling from his eyes, Nobby tried to speak but was overcome by mirth, but then finally got it out. "I'd 'ave paid you a fousand quid to see that!"

Chapter 16

An aide opened the door, uttering exaggerated words of encouragement to a boy of around twelve, but he pulled away defiantly and ran off with the aide hot on his heels.

In the control room, the director watched the painstaking progress.

"Processor is in the hive, no, he's gone… let's go to memory instead."

Making a quarter turn, he leaned over another engineer, and through the glass, another aide could be seen walking in with a young boy of around seven.

"Memory is in the hive… activate the bubble and bring his favorite hologram online."

A holographic display of endlessly connecting pipes hovered over the armrest and drew the child to the recliner where he took his seat, mesmerized by the three-dimensional imagery, and when he sensed the massaging vibration, he sat further back into the seat.

The processor engineer interrupted the director. "He's back, sir." Through the glass, the processor child could be seen inching through the door, but then he pulled back and the door closed shut again. "Sorry, he's gone."

The director took a deep breath. "Okay, go to light show in the processor cell. Begin receptive conditioning sequence for memory, emm, sports trivia, the last one hundred years."

The processor cell's soft, spongy-coated walls changed from

a soft glow to a more stimulating rainbow shower of changing colors. The processor boy peeked into the room, and on this occasion, he was captivated by the wondrous display, and walked in with his aide in tow.

From below the seat, a robotic arm presented a flat-screen at eye-level with an electronic writing template and an attached stylus, to the lap of the memory child. He picked up the stylus, his head tilted to the right and left, and his eyes focus was almost through the display, as it showed a set of scrolling sports questions.

Rapidly, he wrote down answers, to which the system responded, "Good job, Padeen... well done, Padeen."

The director showed growing excitement. "I'm going to need a complete system status on my mark, everyone. Receptive conditioning sequence for the processor, ease the cell lights back, pulse the bubble with a bass rhythm, and a scent of lavender. Let's get him good to go."

The processor boy turned his head toward the bubble in the center of the room in response to the sound of the bass. The cell lights returned to a soft glow and the boy's nose turned up and his head twitched as he detected the scent. He took a circuitous route to the bubble and climbed slowly into his seat. Willing on the child with every fiber of his body, the director said, "Okay, that's it, go on, go... okay, let me have a biological computer status, mark?"

The engineers reported in sequence:

"Output, ready to go online."

"Input, ready to go online."

"Processor, in the bubble."

"Memory, ready to go online."

The processor child settled himself further in his seat, and a robotic arm presented a flat-screen at eye level and an electronic writing template to his lap with a stylus that he took in his hand.

"Yes! Yes!" the director exclaimed, and then quickly composed himself. "Right, okay… receptive conditioning sequence for the processor, give him something basic to begin with."

The processor child watched the screen as a rolling set of high-level calculus questions appeared on the screen, to which he wrote answers at an inconceivable speed without hesitation, and in response, the system responded with, "Hey, that was great, Freidrich … you got it right, Freidrich."

Chapter 17

The city should have been deserted at midnight but it buzzed with activity. It was somewhat expected to see nurses, maintenance personnel, hospitality staff, and delivery drivers, but ordinary Londoners were night owls, and many used this time to run personal errands, shop, socialize and exercise. There was also a large number of tourists who loved the diversity and vibrancy of the city and none were restricted by transportation because the underground tube, overground railway, and busses ran through the night.

Helen's offices were empty except for the cleaners and few paid any attention as James and Helen unlocked and entered her office. Opening the medical cabinet, she used a flashlight to read the labels, and pocketed several vials and syringes. Leaving her office and locking it behind them, they scanned up and down the corridors, leaving quickly and disappearing into the night.

***

Surbiton's train station in Surrey could not have been more diametrically opposite to Devon's St. Clements station.

Constructed in the 1930s, it must have shocked passengers at the time to see the traditional brickwork, which had always began as red, and went to black over time due to the steam engine's soot, be replaced with a white façade. But since non-polluting electric trains were to be the future, it was quite practical for this Modernist concrete canopy to be painted white.

It was early evening and Gregory Kerry and a number of other well-heeled commuters exited the train, walked down the platform, and left the station through the large ticket hall.

Crossing the high street, Kerry went past a row of closed shops and then cut across the park green. He had the strange sense that he was being watched but he shrugged off the sensation as he was sure the only person it could be would not make the same mistake twice.

As he left the park, a cab was waiting at the exit, engine running, empty with the 'for hire' light off. Nobby and Helen stepped out from behind to block his path.

Helen lifted her hands in a gesture to have him stop. "I would like to ask again for your help, please, Mr. Kerry."

Looking over his shoulder, but seeing nobody, he smirked sarcastically. "Didn't you learn your lesson… this conversation is over."

Emerging quickly from behind, James walked directly at Kerry, who swung his briefcase at him. Dropping to a knee, the case flew over his head as James jabbed a syringe into his thigh and depressed the plunger. Kerry dropped to the ground in pain, and James leaned over him snapping, " Damn right it's over!"

***

It was early evening and in the center of the medieval walled town of Sant Joan, we saw an eighteenth-century church encircled by cobble-stoned streets stretching out like a web in all directions. The streets are lined with bushes of oleander, bougainvillea, honeysuckle, and almond and olive trees. People moved along in a parade, dressed as devils and skeletons, carrying pitchforks with fireworks attached which they set off while dancing to the rhythmic beats of music and drums. Bonfires burned on beaches, in villages and towns, and family and friends gathered together to eat and drink around the fire, throwing in firecrackers.

The aunts were seated at a café, watching all this gaiety with great fascination, accompanied by a distinguished-looking, older Spanish gentleman.

May looked on with confusion. "What are they writing on those pieces of paper, Vicente, because they keep making mistakes and throwing them into the fire?"

Vicente smiled. "They are writing down their wishes or sins and burning them in the hope of manifesting or absolving them. The fire is a symbol of purification, to drive the evil spirits away."

May seemed to have an albeit tenuous hold of the plot and took time to follow up. "That explains the Joan of Arc reference."

Vicente looked completely confused, but Rose was very much used to her sister's ways. "This is nothing to do with Joan of Arc, May, Sant Joan is Saint John in Spanish."

"Ah, that makes even more sense then. It seemed strange they should celebrate an English Saint."

"She wasn't English, May, she was French."

"Of course she wasn't, Rose, I saw the movie all about her on the television, and there weren't any captions."

Rose decided to leave that where it stood, but May had more questions. "But you said it was a religious celebration, Vicente?"

"It was originally a pagan celebration to mark the beginning of summer solstice, but the Catholic Church marks it as the birth of John the Baptist."

"I see," said May, her face looking befuddled.

Rose was not so encumbered by these practicalities and was

clapping her hands to the music. "It's hard to imagine this at St. Clements, don't you think, May?"

May had been picking at the pastries in front of them.

Vicente volunteered an explanation. "These are traditional, this cake is sugar-coated with pieces of candied fruit, pine nuts, and sometimes pork rind. This puff pastry is called Coca de Recapte, it has baked peppers and eggplant, and improved with sardines, herrings or sausage."

May returned the cake to the tray. "Very nice, I'm sure." Picking up her cocktail, she took a sip. "And what is this cocktail you ordered for us, Vicente?"

"Blood juice freeze."

May's face attempted a smile through cringing horror.

Chapter 18

While Nobby drove through the night, James and Helen sat on either side of Kerry, as his head drooped and his eyes rolled back into his head.

James was rifling through his briefcase, and pulled out an address book, but then looked at their near-unconscious informant with disappointment.

"This truth serum has just knocked him out, Helen... I thought he'd be more receptive."

"That's movie magic - sodium pentathol produces a state of full relaxation, making him more susceptible to suggestion, but he won't tell us anything if he doesn't want to."

Nobby had the sliding window open. "What're you eating back there?"

"It's the drug Nobby," Helen answered, "it has a garlic-like odor... talking about food, can we get something? I'm famished."

"Leave the grub to me, Helen."

James shook the now-slumped Kerry and tried to bring him round with a slap to the face.

"That won't work, James. I gave him a slightly heavier dose, otherwise, he'd be conscious... let me do this." Taking a deep breath to relax her voice, she said, "Gregory... Gregory, I'm going to ask you some questions. Can you hear me?"

He replied in a groggy slur. "No, I can't hear you."

"What about James Moore?"

Kerry did not respond but closed his eyes.

Lifting an eyelid, Helen could see them moving rapidly, indicating a brain response. Seeing this, James paused for a moment, and then asked Nobby, "How long will it take to get to Heathrow?"

"Twenny minutes tops."

"Let's go."

When they got closer, Nobby leaned back. "Where abouts did you want to go, Jimmy?"

Helen smiled, looking at James. "Yes, Jimmy, where did you want to go?"

James shook his head smiling back at her in acceptance. "The lockers please, Nobby."

"They're at all the terminals."

"These were near a rather ugly sculpture of boards standing up and painted badly with geometric shapes."

"Good, I know exactly where that is. They use those unique sculptures on purpose, you know, to herd us."

James came out of the terminal's sliding doors carrying two backpacks and climbed into the waiting taxi.

"Can you find us somewhere quiet to park, Nobby?"

"Right you are."

Seating himself opposite, he hooked up the Mind Link system and placed the primary headset on Kerry, who was still in a semi-conscious state.

James explained his rationale. "He can control what he says, but he can't control what he thinks."

James placed the repeating headset on himself, and after stopping on a quiet street, Nobby turned in his seat to get a better view. "Are you going to electrocute his brain?"

"No, this gear will let me get inside his head."

"I could just hook the jumper cable up to the car battery and cook him a little. That'll wake 'is ideas up!"

"Nice idea, Nobby, and I appreciate the enthusiasm, but let's start with this."

James prepared the Mind Link, and then activated the system. "Ask him the same question when I'm in, Helen."

As expected, inside the mind of Kerry were stacks of lenticular screens, stacked in a time lapsed order. The drug-induced waking sleep made for a disjointed journey as he went in and out of memories and James witnessed random visions of Oxford, a nude woman, a warm sunny beach, but in no chronological order. They stabilized for only a short time, giving no time to decipher their location, time index, or connection.

Helen's voice could be heard. "What do you know of James Moore?"

This triggered a quick transition to a memory which showed a man playing racket ball with Kerry. It was a friendly game and there appeared to be a bond between them, as they made a reference to their college days at Oxford. This friend had an American accent. "This comes from a high tier, Greg, so get with the beat baggy!"

"I'll get right on it, Jeff. What's he done? Do you know?"

"Who knows? But it ain't good, that's for sure. Hate to be in his shoes."

James prompted Helen. "Ask him about an American named Jeff."

Kerry's mind navigated the memory access and we saw a large sequence of nude women, who appeared to be prostitutes, taking payment indifferently, as Kerry unsuccessfully tried to engage them in conversation after the act.

Helen tried the trigger. "What about Jeff, the American?"

A new series of scenes were then accessed in which we saw a younger Jeff reach out to shake Kerry's hand, saying "Welcome to the Collective." There was another scene in which Jeff and his wife, apparently, arrived at the airport on a visit to England. Kerry greeted them both warmly, and then a memory jump occurred and we saw Jeff in a quiet corner of a restaurant troubled, with Kerry.

"I'm fucked, Greg."

"What've you done?"

"Inside trading. It was stupid, but we get access to such key information, I couldn't resist it."

"But why? You didn't need to. Not with the Collective."

"I got greedy, overextended myself." His eyes filled with tears. "I'll lose everything, Emily, my son, they'll take the house in Greenwich."

"Report it back, the Collective can work miracles."

"It's too late, I took a plea bargain. Told them about the Collective to hopefully commute the sentence."

Kerry sat back in his chair in shock. "But, Jeff."

Biting the dry skin around his nails, he said, "I need your help, Greg."

"I can't."

"It's the Department of Justice. They'll protect us... if you back me, we could break this thing. C'mon, it fucked up your life too. You think you're getting away with something, but you know you're a fraud and a cheat. That eats away at you. You said as much, Greg."

Greg said nothing - he just sat back, and then it switched to another scene in which Kerry was alone in his office, pacing the room, fitfully punching one hand into another as he wrestled with something. Sitting down at his desk, he stared at his cell phone for quite some time and then picked it up and texted a message. Almost immediately the phone rang, and he said, "I need to report a breach."

James disconnected the link, and looked at Kerry, still under the drug's influence, but sobbing uncontrollably.

"What's wrong? What's the matter with him, James?"

"He sold his soul, Helen."

***

James and Helen exited the cab at the curb with their few belongings.

Nobby rolled down his window and hung out. Kerry was still out of it, resting peacefully on the back seat.

James shook his hand warmly. "I can't thank you enough Nobby, you saved us."

Helen reached in, kissing and hugging him. "You're a noble soul, Nobby. You've been so kind to us."

The emotion made him more animated. "I don't know what trouble you two are in, but I for one hope you get it sorted."

"Oh!" said James, all at once remembering, pulling out an envelope with the cash, and handing it to him. "I almost forgot."

Nobby raised a rejecting hand. "Keep it, my friends, you're gonna need it." And, pointing a thumb back at Kerry, he called out as he pulled away, "I'll milk sleeping beauty 'ere out of a big fat fare when he comes to!"

Chapter 19

The medical research facility was state-of-the-art and had all the toys a researcher could ever wish for. They had the means to perform complex chemical, biological, hematological, immunologic, and bacteriological tests on a routine basis.

To evaluate these test results, the room had benches loaded with microscopes, incubators, hot and microplates, and autoclaves. The walls were lined with racks of equipment, such as hematology, blood gas, urinalysis, point-of-care and immunoassay analyzers, and differential and gamma counters. It was all within clean rooms with researchers and technicians busy with their tasks, and several attached MRI and CAT scan rooms.

Kirke was the Principal Investigator, and he was a pasty-faced, pudgy man of around forty, with flyaway, thinning hair.

He sat at a workstation, studying brain scans displayed on several monitors, with a hologram projection showing the combination of all in 3D. His desk was in disarray with printouts, sketches and half-finished cups of coffee, and he flitted between screens, finally settling on a table of data presented at the bottom of one of the screens.

A slightly younger Hans approached and Kirke looked up with a twitch, and called out in a naturally grating voice, "Did you get my message, sir, big breakthrough!"

"My good fellow, please call me Hans, and I'm glad to hear it. We have this brand new facility, and I know you have only been with us for two weeks but we expect great things from you,

Dr. Anderson."

"I will do my very best."

"I know you will, and, before I forget, Hannah has a protégé, a twelve-year-old girl named Marianne. I want you to help Hannah develop her into what she needs."

"I will, of course. Can I say again how grateful I am to have been chosen? This is such an opportunity."

"Not at all, young fella. You were the best man for the job... now, what is this breakthrough you mentioned?"

Kirke got up and almost bowed as if to acknowledge the accolades of his achievement. In his mind, an acceptance speech was needed and he began pacing the room in a figure of eight.

"One of the key differences between us and the children is that they choose only one sensory channel, primarily seeing, hearing, or smelling. And this specialization makes that sense very acute."

"I understand, you have mentioned this before... I met a blind girl a few years ago who could walk into a room and, based on the echo she received from her own voice, she could determine the room's dimensions."

"Exactly, they focus on the one sense they favor, and become very adept at using it."

"So... if we could shut down all our senses, but one, we could become a savant."

"No, I am convinced this has nothing to do with it." Kirke lifted his hands to signify accomplishment.

Hans was dumbstruck and confused. "Why are we talking about it then, Kirke?"

"Because I am confident I can eliminate it as a possibility."

"I realize scientists see things differently, but I was hoping we had moved forward... just a little."

"But we have."

"Correct me if I'm wrong, but I see this as a move sideways."

"That's true. I haven't even started down the path I suspect is the right option?"

"And why is that?"

"I thought I'd rule out the wrong paths first?"

"So, what is your favored theory, Kirke?"

"We are not aware of the inner processing of our brain because we subconsciously block it. We are only conscious of the conclusion we draw... the children are aware of the brain's processing and they study the data they bring in with pathological concentration."

"Yes, yes, I understand this."

Kirke activated a simulation showing a child's brain being exposed to three low-level magnetic fields which, in a sweeping 3D view, extend over specific sections of the brain.

"Using carefully timed magnetic pulses, I can inhibit the brain from editing and extracting a conclusion."

Hans pointed to the simulation. "And this will give us savant ability?"

"I think so."

Hans stood to leave. "But you haven't started down this path?"

"No."

"Well, let us pursue this promising path immediately."

"Okay, leave it to me, Hans."

Hans opened the door to leave, hesitated, and turned to Kirke with a chuckle. "And Kirke, don't feel obligated to call me whenever you've found nothing!"

***

The transatlantic flight had dimmed the lights and most of the passengers were already asleep, or well on the way. Helen woke to find James reading a news article on his laptop, with the Mind Link headsets laid out alongside.

Helen immediately reached down for her backpack to verify her legs were still wrapped in the straps. "It's fine, Helen, I haven't let it out of my sight."

"How much did you get out?"

"I closed the account, nearly one hundred and forty six thousand pounds."

"Let's put everything in a lockbox at the airport."

"Sure, love."

Pointing to the laptop, she asked, "Did you find anything?"

"Jeff is Jeff Richardson... and he's dead."

Sitting upright, she asked, "How did it happen?'

"He fell in front of a subway train, from what witnesses describe as a sudden heart attack... but listen to this account from a bystander." James searched for the article, "Ah, here it is... one minute, he was fine, and then he got this phone call, and just collapsed and fell onto the tracks."

"Sounds familiar."

"It does, doesn't it? Maria prevented you from suffering the full effect of whatever it was, and she told Aunt Rose that it has been known to cause permanent damage."

"I don't remember much, other than Maria's scream."

Lifting a headset and handing it to Helen, he said, "I want you to play it back, Helen, using the Mind Link."

"But surely, it will…"

"Don't worry, I have muted the audio so we won't hear a thing, but it will feed straight to the laptop's virtual spectrum analyzer."

"Are you sure it's okay?"

Reassuringly holding her hand, he said, "I'm sure. Start it a little earlier, to test it out so you feel better."

After James and Helen had the mind-link headsets on, Helen returned to the living room when she was talking with Rose, but in this instance, all sound was muted. As the scene played out, we saw Rose lift her hands to her face in excitement, and come over to kiss Helen in a congratulatory way. The link abruptly ended, shut down by Helen, and they were back.

"It's fine, I couldn't hear a thing."

"I'm getting the audio into the analyzer fine... but what were you and Rose..."

"Are you ready?"

"Yes."

Helen navigated to the memory just prior to her receiving the sound spike and the liquid-like lenticular screen enveloped them and they were immersed in it. In almost slow motion, Helen turned, Maria came bursting out the front door, screaming, startling Rose and Helen, and then Helen's view became blurred and she wavered, looking skyward, blinking a few times, and finally blanking out. The link ended and they were back.

"Did you get it?"

James checked. "Yes, it's stored in a buffer. That's interesting, it's centered around thirteen hertz, and looks..." James turned to Helen and smiled. "What were you telling Aunt Rose in the living room?"

"I can't remember."

A knowing silence fell between them, and Helen had to rally to counter James' stare, but her eyes hesitated.

James handed her back the headset. "Mind Link that scene

again - this time we'll do it with sound."

"I don't know what you're talking about James," said Helen playfully. "This is not a good time."

James reached over and kissed her and took both her hands lovingly. "You should've told me, my love... how long?"

"Two months!"

Chapter 20

Entering the first class aisle, Hannah walked briskly past the long line of coach class passengers to a waiting, burly security man who checked her ticket and picture ID. She looked around casually to check for her operatives, strategically separated in the coach class line, dressed casually.

"Is that a laptop, ma'am?"

"Yes, it is."

"It will have to come out of the case."

"Of course."

Moving along, she grabbed two trays for her laptop and shoes. She looked around, noticing this airport had the latest biometrics scanning, passenger tracking, and video surveillance.

Walking through the detector arch, she set off an alarm, and after being waved to the side, a female security guard used her hand wand to determine it was her bracelets.

Looking back impatiently, Hannah could see Marianne had finally decided on her customary two or three pre-flight magazines and was showing her ticket and ID. She was dressed in olive green cargo pants, slung low on the hips, with her signature belt, boots, and a pale yellow, lace camisole top.

Removing her boots and placing them in a tray with her purse, she walked to the arch and waited her turn. When signaled to go through, she was about to walk but stopped abruptly in a gesture of forgetfulness, quickly removed her belt, and with a plaintive, almost coy expression, questioned the guard facing her as to whether she should return to have it scanned. He came willingly to her rescue, took the belt, and was rewarded with an inadvertent hug as she supposedly tripped.

With a flirtatious smile to the young man, she said, "My belt always sets it off - it's a family heirloom that I can't bear to be parted from."

"Well, then, I'll check it personally for you."

"Thank you, thank you." She leaned in and kissed him on the cheek.

Distracted by its weight and intricate design, it captivated his interest a little more than Marianne liked. "Excuse moi, Mr. guard."

"Yes."

Clutching herself under her bra and causing her bust to spill out a little more from her low-cut top, she asked, "The underwire cups in my lace-up bustier sometimes trigger the alarm also, should I take it off?"

The security guard had a momentary lapse of consciousness, entranced by a combination of what he could presently see, and what his imagination was conjuring up at the prospect. This scene attracted the attention of a supervisor, who looked over to see one of his guards staring, spellbound, at a young woman's breasts.

"Do you need assistance, Pete?"

Pete quickly came to his senses, returned the belt to Marianne, and ushered her away without further delay.

Walking to join the waiting Hannah, Marianne slipped the belt through her pant loops and called back, "Merci, mon cheri!"

***

Greenwich Connecticut was nestled along the Long Island Sound and immediately west of the New York state border. It was a short train ride to downtown Manhattan, making it an easy commute for the well-to-do. It had beaches for swimming, boating, and fishing, and cultural festivals throughout the year in the arts, film, and food.

Downtown had fine dining and upscale niche and high-end brand shops, and the locals were casually dressed in a weekend country clubby way, giving off a thinly veiled, but intentional look of affluence.

Emily Richardson looked very much the same as James and Helen remembered her from Kerry's memory, sitting at a window seat in the coffee shop. She sat alone with a three-year-old, staring unappreciatively at her café latte. If anything, she looked a little leaner, she had dark hair which she swept back continually, and an East-Coast sharpness to her voice as she checked her son.

James and Helen entered and walked directly to her. "Mrs. Richardson?"

She was a million miles away and so came back with a bit of a start. "Yes?"

"My name is Helen, this is my husband, James, we got your address from Gregory Kerry in London. We stopped at your house and your housekeeper said we'd find you here."

With immediate concern, she asked, "Is Greg okay?"

"Oh yes, he's fine."

For a moment, she looked disappointed, but then banished the unkind thought, though not before seeing their looks of confusion.

"A bit heartless, I'm sorry to say, misery loves company. It feels so personal, as though I've been... singled out."

James gestured to the two seats opposite and Emily nodded.

"We were sorry to hear about your husband."

"Thank you… he had a physical two months ago. He was as fit as I am. Between golf, racket ball… and he could go the full hour of spin class."

James leaned forward. "I'm not sure if this will make you feel any better, but we're convinced your husband did not have a heart attack, but, in fact, was murdered."

With a look of relief, she said, "I don't know if 'better' is the word, but, strange as it may seem, it does put my mind at ease."

Helen continued, "We're trying to track down the people responsible, for this and other crimes, and wondered if you knew why anyone would want to kill your husband?"

"Yes, but…" she collected her things, and whispered, "…not here, can you come back to the house?"

Chapter 21

The Richardson home was a stone house, built high with a view of Long Island Sound and, on a clear day, Manhattan. They entered a grand entry hall, with a large, formal living room and a dining room to the left and right respectively, and further down, a kitchen was attached to a family room on one side, with an adjacent office further down. Continuing on, a sun-filled hallway connected to the mudroom and a four-car garage.

Emily took them straight to the kitchen and put her son in a high chair with snacks and positioned her phone to display child entertainment. The fully-equipped kitchen featured onyx countertops and expansive, metal-framed picture windows overlooking the rear gardens. She slid open pocket doors that could be closed to screen the catering areas for more formal entertaining.

"I wonder why she closed these." Pointing to a cappuccino machine, she asked, "Would you like a coffee?"

"Yes please, thank you," said Helen, and they sat down at a small breakfast table in an alcove.

"Jeff was obsessed with gain. It's a mandatory requirement for the city, you know. I paid little attention to his business as long as my lifestyle was not interfered with. And then, shortly before he died, we were getting ready to meet friends at the country club and he just broke down and sobbed uncontrollably. He finally pulled himself together, but not before he mentioned something about inside trading, being ruined, and that exposing a secret cooperative organization was the only option."

She delivered the coffee. "He said we'd have to enter the witness protection program and leave. Now I think of it, I stupidly said…" her voice broke, "…I couldn't have my schedule disrupted. I bike, you see - and that's when he stopped, said pressures at work had been tiring him, and we went out and it was never mentioned again."

She noticed some dishes that had not been washed and cleaning items which had been left out.

"Please excuse the mess… Sonia! Sonia! Let's go through to the living room. I insist one room is not used by anyone and so it's always spotless!"

Entering the living room, Emily was surprised to see a French door's glass pane broken and the door wide open.

James walked over to check outside.

Emily called again, this time with a hint of irritability. "What on earth has happened here? Sonia, Sonia!"

Hannah, Marianne, and two operatives walked quickly in behind them. One operative grabbed Helen, while the other held Emily.

Hannah raised her hands to signal for James to stop. "Our orders are to acquire, not kill…" she said and, pointing to a bloody pool encircling a body in the dining room, added, "…Mrs. Richardson's maid, Sonia, I think you said, couldn't be relied on to remain silent."

Emily was sobbing uncontrollably, and Hannah nodded to Marianne who walked to her son, removed her Tri-blade, and sat near him on the sofa.

"Now, Emily, can we rely on your silence, or is this to play out as a tragic sequel to the Richardson family's demise?"

Emily stifled her crying with her hand. "Please, please, I will do anything you ask."

Helen was held securely, but her eyes met James', and a message passed between them. Her eyes were filled with tears, and he shook his head slightly to reject the idea.

Helen's eyes flicked to the French doors and the woods beyond.

James' eyes narrowed in defiance, and then Helen's lips mouthed "Please,"

With a begrudging shrug, he turned quickly and ran straight through the door. They were all taken aback by this unforeseen tactical move and Hannah seemed speechless for a few seconds, but recovered to shout to the operatives, "Get him! We can deal with them."

***

James ran past the glass-walled pool house and down a slope and around the ruins of a former party pavilion. The grass was manicured to perfection and there were several areas shaded by mature maple trees. He leaped over several flower beds and shrubs and skirted a vegetable and fruit garden. Reaching the perimeter of the lot, a sign at a padlocked gate read, 'Greenwich Audubon Society' and so he hurdled the fence.

He entered a natural area, with an abundance of wildflowers and interesting granite rock outcrop formations. Jogging alongside a healthy stream and vernal ponds, he could see a wetland meadow to his right and a red maple swamp to his left. He stuck to the trail for now, although this predictability was dangerous.

Where to hide. Go to ground or keep going?

A hillside wetland and emergent freshwater marsh were not ideal, and this was encircled by a wetland scrub thicket.

Stay on the trail, he told himself, and see what opportunity presents itself.

The landscape changed to reveal deep, shady gorges below a canopy of mature oak, beech, and maple trees, a grove of white pines, and deep shady ravines.

This is more like it, he thought, this is like being at home.

Some light made it through the canopy to paint patches of yellow on the leafy ground, and his heightened senses could hear the cries of birds and small mammals as echoes since these sounds were unable to escape the density of the woodland. He searched the landscape as a beam of light being refracted by dew droplets on a leaf caught his eye.

The muddied and sweating operatives were weaving their way slowly through the undergrowth, but they slowed as they stopped periodically to listen. They traveled in two separate but parallel trails to widen the search area, but they could still see each other and were able to send visual cues. In their dark suits and dress shoes, they were not suited for the task at hand and already looked worse for wear. They had discovered many different footprints traveling in all directions but without knowing which were James', they were none the wiser.

Helen sat sandwiched between Hannah and Marianne in the backseat of a moving car. Helen stared ahead with an uncooperative cold and distant air, while Marianne studied her with interest.

Hannah was in her familiar command and control role.

An operative could be heard reporting his frustration, and Helen smiled. Hannah ignored this.

"I'll access your phones to get your position, hold on, I have another call… Yes, I want to activate a collective alert for the surrounding area, I want law enforcement, hunters, even bird enthusiasts… I need as much help as I can get."

Chapter 22

A large deputation had arrived at the original New England homestead buildings which had an apple orchard to the west and surrounding stone walls.

The sanctuary director had climbed onto an overturned delivery box and was determined to give a speech. "I'd like to thank all of you for coming. The wetland meadows have a huge variety of plant species - tussock sedges, cattails, and pink lady slipper orchids. In the fall and spring migration, this area is an excellent birding spot."

Hannah interrupted. "This is not why you are here."

He carried on, ignoring her. "The trails will lead you to hardwood forests, old fields, lakes, streams, and vernal pools. In the ever-expanding urbanization, our sanctuary serves as a haven for a wide variety of other wildlife, as well as birds."

Hannah walked up to a senior law enforcement officer. "Get rid of him and anyone else who will stand in our way." Shaking her head, she returned to her car, muttering to herself, "I knew the bird watcher group was a bad idea," and then into her headset, she said, "Report."

"Our phones are on and so we should be visible."

James was on a flat and open clearing, and vulnerable. He had carefully scraped away a layer of leaves and dug out a shallow trench with a rock. The dirt and rocks had been put carefully into his jacket, tying the sleeves and walking across rocks to empty it into a deep puddle. The spot had been carefully selected and when he was satisfied, he crossed the rocks one more time and then walked backward, placing his feet carefully in previous footprints. Using a broom-shaped stick to even out the leaves as he backed into the recess, he first covered himself with some of the remaining dirt and then with leaves, flattening them as he moved up his body to be sure he was landscape level before putting his head down and pulling the last over his now fully camouflaged body.

Two deep breaths in, one slow breath out, two in, one out...

Hannah studied the map on her laptop with the moving red dots and its associated ID. A report came in: "No sign of him yet, but from the tracks we had at the river, we know he came this way, ma'am."

"He doesn't know where he's going, but he knows where he came from... my guess is he'll double back, so stay sharp."

"We're on a flat open clearing at the moment... nowhere to hide here, ma'am, so we're moving quickly past this area."

Inside his trench, James had slowed down his system to a point of peaceful relaxation. On seeing the operative pass by, however, he was wide awake and he turned his head very slightly left and then to the right until he heard the accomplice moving past along a high ridge.

Hannah studied the display thoughtfully and caught Helen watching it too. "We will get him."

"Good luck... he is highly inventive. He will outwit and outmaneuver you at every turn."

A new red dot and identifier appeared at the top of the screen. This was followed by a second, third, fourth, and then a rapid filling of the screen's perimeter with nearly thirty converging dots.

Hannah was relieved. "Ah, the cavalry... go to a high point

and hold your position, I think he's gone to ground."

Helen tried not to be concerned about the now overwhelming odds. A second phone rang and Hannah reached into her handbag, answered it but said nothing to the caller, and then, "It's for you."

Taken aback, Helen hesitated before taking the phone and lifting it to her ear.

Hans was on the line. "Ms. Thompson? Oh, I'm sorry, Mrs. Moore, please forgive me. Can you hear me?"

Hearing howling dogs in the distance, James climbed out of his trench and jogged back to the river, immersed himself in the icy water to wash away scent, and moved downstream as fast as he could, looking for a suitable exit point.

Helen hesitated before answering, "Yes."

"It is important you understand that I wish no harm to come to the two of you, but accidents do happen in these circumstances my dear, so I'm imploring you to listen to me and not escalate this any further."

"Go on."

"If you give me your word not to try anything foolish until I have had a chance to explain, in person, I will call off the hunt for Mr. Moore."

Helen glanced at the map on Hannah's laptop display, which showed an ever-tightening circle of red dots.

A group of hunters reached James' fox hole and the dogs nosed through it in a crisscrossing pattern, and then tore off down the incline in a howling frenzy.

James had run from one stream to another and reversed course to go upstream, but the dogs were not fooled. They were on him faster than he imagined they could be, so he ducked down in the water and hid under a rock overhang short of options. After a back-and-forth frantic search, the dogs found him, and the men stood staring at him - James realized the game was up.

Helen showed extreme anguish, as she looked again at the map on Hannah's laptop to see all of the individual red dots clustered and almost indistinguishable.

"Okay, agreed."

The soaked and dripping James emerged from the river with a thoroughly confused look on his face. He stood motionless at the water's edge, watching the hunting parties walk away. He recognized the operative he had eluded earlier and stared at him until his gaze was sensed and he turned. The operative shook his head and smiled, slowly lifted his arm, shaped his hand into a gun, rotated it slowly as if to savor the moment, and reflexed his wrist to simulate firing.

Chapter 23

Hannah parked her car and paused to admire the beautiful Swiss valley dotted with shepherd huts and to take in the therapeutic sound of cowbells. The Kääferberg Sauna was just outside a village of the same name, and adjacent to a tributary which cascaded down to eventually flow into the Rhine. More than a century ago, the sauna's location had been chosen not by accident, but by design, when a natural hot spring had been diverted for therapeutic bathing, and what followed had been an accompanying luxury hotel to complete the full-service resort.

Hannah entered the spacious and elegant lobby, and on seeing her arrive, the general manager stepped lively from behind the reception desk to greet her personally.

"A pleasure to see you again, madam. Welcome back!"

"Hello, Gunther."

"Everything is prepared as you requested."

Not missing a step on her way to the spa, she said, "I'm expecting Miss Dufay, send her on will you."

"Miss Dufay is already here, in the main bath."

Hannah continued, waved a thank you and left him behind, entering a short, enclosed passage designed to disconnect the guest from the outside world through two ninety-degree knight's turns, and as she emerged to brightness, a gentle trickle of water could be heard from several ancient-looking faucets emptying into a cascading set of small pools. From this upper level, she was afforded a view of the main pool which opened to a spectacular semicircular view of the valley. Horizontally laid stone seats were interspersed with vertical stone pillars which surrounded the pool, and as she descended the stairs, she scanned the right-wing containing showers and steam rooms and the changing rooms to the left. A crescent gap in the roof allowed a half-moon shape of light to play on the surface of the water and part of the stone floor.

Nudity was accepted but did not prevail, with most of the occupants in swimsuits and bath robes. Hannah spotted Marianne standing at the bar with a cocktail, surrounded by four young men. She was dressed in a yellow bikini with black polka dots, and the halter top had an exquisite button detail. The bikini bottom had a low-rise over which she was wearing her signature tri-blade belt. The young men seem happy for Marianne to endlessly explain the cut and style of her swimsuit as it afforded them the legitimacy to study, at close quarters, what the bikini barely concealed.

Marianne spotted Hannah approaching. "Ma cheri!"

"We have a Thai massage and private sauna booked and they are awaiting us."

Grabbing her Louis Vuitton purse, she said, "Sorry boys, I have to go."

One young man stepped forward, reluctant to let Marianne get away.

"Maybe we could meet for dinner, later?"

Marianne looked to Hannah, to the young man, and then back to Hannah. The young man was not willing to give up.

"And of course, please bring your mother!"

Marianne bit her bottom lip and smiled cheekily choking off a laugh, as Hannah took her by the arm, and pulled her away.

***

Like many European cities, it was easy to trace the medieval urban outline of Zürich. Its city center and green spaces encircled Lake Zürich, with beautiful parks connecting up to Zurich Mountain. The modern sections of the city had theaters, nightlife, galleries, and high-end stores, whereas the Old City center, 'Altstadt' had the main train station, trolleys, historical architecture and a selection of the country's renowned chocolate, watch, and jewelry trademarks.

The narrow cobblestone streets in the center of Alstadt emptied into a square with a fountain in its center. It was a warm and sunny day and the beautifully restored medieval houses lining the perimeter were now home to art galleries, boutiques, quaint restaurants, hotels, and antique shops. In a small coffee house, Hans and Hannah sat quietly with a pot of coffee.

Hannah appeared subdued, and distant in her manner. "I had him, you shouldn't have stopped me."

Hans took a sip of coffee. "It is more important to start off on the right foot."

"You would have been in a better position to negotiate."

"I didn't want to negotiate, I would prefer they voluntarily cooperate. And now we have her, he will be along shortly. Ensure his path to us is a smooth one."

Hannah stirred her coffee loudly and with unnecessary force. "Overall, I would say it went well."

He watched her expectantly. "I wouldn't."

Snapping back, she asked, "Why?"

"You were warned of his abilities, had an inside informant, and the element of surprise. It should have been cleaner."

"He was lucky."

"Twice?"

Looking away, she was too overwhelmed to answer.

"You give your best to others, and you're worst to me."

Hans took her hand and tried to kiss it, but she pulled it away disobediently. He smiled at how characteristic this conversation with her was.

"My darling, stop it. You solicited my opinion, and I do hate wasting the resources of the Collective to clean up operations that could have been avoided."

"I didn't want your opinion - it doesn't matter."

"It does if you're upset."

"Lukas died and so he didn't have the opportunity to disappoint you."

"You don't disappoint me."

Hannah was stunned for a moment, unable to answer. She looked away to conceal a tear and saw Helen arriving, escorted by an operative. "You'll have your work cut out for you with this one… she's as stubborn as he is."

Helen entered as Hannah left, and Hans stood to greet her.

"I thought we'd get a drink and walk if that's okay with you, Mrs. Moore?"

"That's fine."

"Can I offer you something? I recommend the hot Swiss chocolate, it's almost sinful."

"Just a coffee with milk, please."

Collecting their drinks, Helen watched with interest as Hans waved away the operative keeping pace behind, and they strolled along a shaded promenade to the quays where pleasure boats were out to enjoy the weather on the lake. Many passers-by called out a friendly greeting to Hans.

"To travel these old streets is to follow in the footsteps of

Charlemagne, Goethe, Einstein, and Lenin... some of the oldest houses date from the 1100s."

Helen managed a false smile.

"How stupid of me. I'm sorry, my dear, to enter into such irrelevant small talk."

Helen somewhat warmed to his honesty. "No, it's okay."

"I wish I knew how to begin, maybe, if you wouldn't mind, would you go first?"

"I would be happy to. Where is James, and is he okay?"

"He is fine, and has traveled to Copenhagen?"

"Copenhagen?"

"Yes... he is a resourceful fellow - I do look forward to meeting him... he is hot on your trail."

Helen studied Hans with confused curiosity, and on seeing this, he continued with a chuckle. "Please don't stop now; we're moving along famously."

"What is the Collective?"

"Straight to the point, my dear, I like that. It was an SS officer who first proposed the idea as a reverse-logic strategy. If you can't conquer a nation from the outside in, try beating them from the inside out. The Hitler-youth children from Ordensburg University were evacuated to Argentina at the end of the war, and they made up the Fahnenbrueder group. It was this group that initiated the creation of the Collective... but let us not dwell on details so far in the past. The key point is, that what was conceived by evil, I have converted for the common good."

Helen shook her head in disbelief at this last comment, and at first was too overwhelmed to respond, but then stopped to face him.

"Good? Good? I think you may be clinically delusional."

Hans seemed hurt for a moment by her unkindness and

looked off to the mountains beyond the lake before responding.

"We recruit young men and women who show enormous promise, and at present, there are just over two hundred and seventy thousand people in the Collective. In the next decade, some of our members will be in a position to prevent wars and promote a cooperative global community for the good of humanity. At present, we fund a large percentage of the world's charities and research facilities that work tirelessly in search of cures for human suffering... We can only hope in our lifetime to do more right than wrong. I'd hoped I could somehow make you understand, Mrs. Moore."

"James and I have been on the wrong side of your organization for some time now, and we haven't seen much in the way of any good."

"Then I must remedy that, you are right."

After a pause, she asked, "You assure me James will not be harmed?"

"You have my word, and since actions speak louder than words, I will grant you access to our facility and I want you to put me to the test!"

"I certainly will..." And then she smiled kindly and extended her hand. "... and you must call me Helen."

Chapter 24

James eventually found the right lecture hall at The University of Copenhagen and entered through the large doors. It had new wooden flooring, energy-efficient LED lighting and a custom acoustic ceiling. He stepped down past the tiered seating and noticed that they had renovated everything except the historic double-height arched stone windows which had been restored beautifully, but looked incongruous with their automatic shades.

On hearing him approach, an older man seated at the desk on the podium looked up from having had his head in his hands, reading. He was around sixty, wiry and his voice carried irritation, and even his mannerisms conveyed an intrinsic bitterness. "Lecture is over, you missed it."

James continued, "Professor Dufay?"

Without hesitation, he replied, "And you must be James Moore, I presume."

James stopped and searched the empty room nervously.

Dufay continued in a bored, impatient manner. "Your wife is at the Savant Foundation just outside Zurich. Mr. Hans Langsdorf wanted me to let you know no harm has come to her, and he would like to meet you in person to explain."

James paused for a moment and Dufay shrugged his shoulders to question why James was not leaving.

"Thank you."

"You're welcome."

As James climbed the stairs, Dufay called out, "As a matter

of interest, how did you arrive at me?"

"My wife was exposed, through her phone, to a sound burst, sweeping through a range centered at thirteen hertz. An internet search revealed your colleague, Kirke Albertsen, was researching the physiological effects resulting from external stimuli matching the brain's natural frequency."

"I see... is this being used as a weapon?"

"I believe so. From what I can tell, it has the same effect as the old disco strobe lights that induced epileptic shock. This uses a sound burst that sweeps through the band and when its frequency matches the recipient's natural resonant brain wave frequency, it induces a synaptic shock."

"How disappointing. Kirke was a graduate student of mine... you will also find him at the Savant Foundation. Mind you, who am I to judge - hypocrisy is rife."

James hesitated to respond to such a personal comment. "Thanks for your help."

Waving his hand in a sweeping away motion, he mumbled as James left. "Yes, yes. Beware of those who cloak their actions with good intentions. Vigilance, Mr. Moore."

***

Hans was in his office, indulging in his favored pastime, the repair of an antique Swiss timepiece. He placed the extracted mechanism in a small bath of cleaning liquid and activated the ultrasonic vibrating pool.

There was a gentle knock at the door and James entered, accompanied by Hans' secretary.

Long, Edwardian-style windows on either side of his desk showed that it was snowing, gently, and a comfortable sofa and two chairs in the seating area were illuminated by the flicker of a generous log fire. Removing his magnifying eyepiece, he rose quickly, crossing the room to shake James' hand, and motioned toward the seating. "Can I offer you some tea, Mr. Moore? I understand you favor Earl Grey?"

James looked tired and as he searched the room, disappointed. "Thank you."

Hans knew what he wanted. "Your charming wife has been assisting us with our children here, I have sent word for her to join us."

Taking a seat opposite, James said, "I appreciate that."

A tray of tea was brought in and Hans lifted another tray, containing the inner workings of an eighteenth-century timepiece.

"My passion, one of them, at least."

"Swiss-made calibers are exemplary. They were way ahead of their time in micro-mechanical engineering."

"My dear fellow, it makes me so happy to hear you say that. Few people have an appreciation. In the early 1800s, these old watchmakers like La Chaux-de-Fonds, Le Loc, and Saint-Imier produced such mechanisms, and here we are, three centuries later, and the Swiss are still untouchable."

"It is interesting to me that such a wealth of innovation could come from such a small group of people. The chronograph, tachymeter, depth alarm, date window, moon phase, their developments with battery reserve, the annual calendar, dual time, the list goes on and on."

"They seemed to spur each other on, a sort of innovation epicenter if you will."

"I agree. The more talented your colleagues, the more it appears to bring out the best in you."

"But surely, Mr. Moore, timing is everything."

"Yes, time seems to be in almost every formula, making it the single most important element in life. But what good is timing without talent?"

"But what good is ability without opportunity?"

"True, but in my experience, talent will prevail no matter what the obstacles."

"Have you ever wondered how much talent is wasted?"

"Whenever a student of mine dropped out, I felt the loss keenly, and always believed they would have had a much more rewarding life if they had only stayed the course."

"I can understand that... if I could offer you anything, anything in life, what would you wish for?"

James looked at Hans but said nothing.

"A dream job offer, a recording contract, financial windfall... a publisher for that novel in you... most people have a small circle of family and friends, a limited network. The Collective is a global resource whose members, by the very nature of their academic excellence, have advanced into positions of great influence."

"You don't see this as corrupt?"

"Would you offer an opportunity to a friend or a stranger first?"

Their discussion was interrupted by the arrival of Helen and, after she and James had embraced, they took a seat opposite Hans, who offered to pour Helen tea, which she accepted.

"Under my direction, the Collective is employed for the good of mankind."

"What about Jeff Richardson, would he agree? By the way, are his wife and child still alive?"

"His wife and child are very well and will be provided for.

Mr. Richardson intended to destroy the Collective for his own selfish ends. Our medical research budget alone is greater than that of most industrialized nations. It would be criminally negligent to allow someone to destroy the discoveries we are on the brink of uncovering in genetic cures, cancer, and so much more… no, the welfare of the many has to outweigh the loss of a few bad seeds."

Helen pulled out of this vein. "What do you want of us?"

Slapping his knee, he said, "Helen, you are right, my dear, let me get to the point. The two of you are ideally suited to collaborate with me to further the good we are trying to achieve. Helen, you have seen how much help we need with our gifted autistic children and Mr. Moore, would you mind if I called you James?"

"By all means."

"We would be so honored to have you help us with our research."

James and Helen were taken aback somewhat, and after glancing at each other, James was about to speak but was beaten to it by Hans.

"No, no. I realize this is a big decision, and I want you to take all the time you need. I have organized an apartment for you in the residential wing. Take your time, investigate what we are doing. I want you both to have complete freedom, but… please, give me your word, that you will not leave without first seeing me."

James leaned forward. "I can assure you, we are going nowhere until we resolve this."

Chapter 25

It was a strange feeling to leave Hans's office, for James to be given a map of the foundation and a list of contact numbers which Helen already had, and then to be set free to go wherever they chose. They had each voluntarily given their word not to escape, but to conduct their own due diligence for however long they felt was needed. Helen took James on a brief tour of the Savant Foundation, and since it had been a long and nerve-wracking few days, they retired early to the luxury apartment they had been assigned.

It was a dwelling intent on providing its occupants with a higher than average amount of comfort, convenience, and quality. Its floor-to-ceiling windows allowed in a large amount of natural light, and large and high spaces provided a sense of grandeur. Luxurious furnishing spoiled you for choice of which room to enjoy, a rooftop infinity pool, private movie theatre, gymnasium, and wine cellar accessorized the splendor. The kitchen had every appliance conceivable with extensive granite and marble, the bedroom had a double king-size bed, a full walk-in closet, and spacious, spa-like bathrooms.

While Helen cooked a light meal, James covered the apartment from floor to ceiling looking for bugging devices but found none - which somehow didn't make him feel better at all.

In the early morning hours, he twisted and turned in his sleep, their day had agitated his mind and it wrestled to defragment…

Two Super Etendard strike fighters completed a mid-air refueling from a KC-130h tanker, banked east, and dropped to a lower altitude. The south Atlantic had a high wind shear, and a heavy swell spawned waves that rolled over great distances to collide with surface waves. H.M.S. Sheffield was having a hard time of it - ten hundred hours, May the second, 1982. A younger James in officer's uniform was making his way through the ship to salutes and friendly calls from shipmates as he passed.

The jets skimmed dangerously low over the choppy sea at five hundred feet. The lead pilot's attention flicked between his altimeter and radar, and at first, there was nothing, and then three targets popped up at twenty-five miles. Handing off these coordinates to the weapons system, the jets dropped to an even lower level to evade the ship's radar, and after a last-minute check, he and his wingman launched their AM39 Exocet missiles.

The missiles dropped like dead weights until their engines engaged and they thrust forward, sending up a fine sea spray wake, hurtling towards the ships at one thousand, one hundred and thirty kilometers per hour. The jets banked, slowly maintaining their low altitude, and headed home to their base in Argentina. The missiles' onboard guidance and control systems dropped them to an even lower altitude.

A radar operator in H.M.S. Sheffield's command-information-center (CIC) picked up a faint blip on the radar, ignored it, and then a little later it reappeared at a very close range, and he reported the sighting in an almost unintelligible babble. The first missile passed within one hundred feet of H.M.S. Yarmouth, as this was not its intended target, dropped to its final altitude of six feet, and went straight for the Sheffield.

James was picked up like a rag doll and slammed against a bulkhead as the missile hit with tremendous force. The ringing in his ears blocked all other noise, and a head wound blurred his vision, disabling him for what seemed like an eternity. The ship rolled heavily and he rolled with it, sliding back and forth in the passage. Lighting dimmed, came back, shut down, and finally switched to emergency backup. Personnel ran past him in a blur, and his emotions were in a state of complete chaos. The ship's roll had settled now but she was listing, and he struggled to his feet, only to quickly duck as ammunition storage fires caused rounds to cook off.

There were dead bodies and mutilated body parts everywhere, and the CIC was not there anymore - replaced by a gaping hole with fires burning out of control. He made his way towards the bridge, wiping blood from his eyes. The ship had gone to battle stations but there was none of the usual order of drills, the remaining ship's company were in a state of panic, all training forgotten. Standing in knee-high water, he reached an integrated-ships-instrumentation-system panel, and then was approached by a young ensign. "Sir? Sir?"

"Status, Mr. Reade?"

James continued towards the bridge, followed by Reade, as straining steel groaned, water gushed and pipes burst all around adding to the fray, and the young man flinched as he reported. "The engine room is flooding and on fire, and the missiles spent fuel has spread the fire faster than we can control it."

"Senior officers?"

"CIC was destroyed... you are the highest ranking officer I have found alive, sir."

"Let us get to the bridge then."

The bridge stations were manned by scared seamen who watched as he arrived, and pleaded with their eyes for an answer as to, why? A phone rang and Reade answered it. "Engineering,

Lieutenant Pullings, sir."

James took the phone. "Stephen, it's James, what happened to the anti-fire system?"

"We lost both primary and secondary electric power."

"Then get out of there."

"The fire has trapped us... and we are flooding at an alarming rate. How much are we listing?"

Checking the instruments, he frowned and was reluctant to say, "Ten degrees to starboard and fifteen degrees by the stern... I'm coming down."

"Stay there! there's not a lot we can do... you know, aluminum will burn. We should have stayed with steel ships. Speed over safety will be judged as a bad choice."

A long pause was heard in which the crackle on the line was accentuated.

"...James, things are pretty hopeless down here... I've got to go."

"Stephen, Stephen?"

The line went dead.

The vibrant and energetic Sheffield which had been so alive moments earlier, lay motionless and set at an unnatural angle having received her mortal wound. Reade and the rest of the bridge staff stared at James in anticipation of the order they were willing him to utter.

To himself, checking the radar, he said, "Who is the closest - Arrow or Yarmouth?" James picked up the ship-to-ship phone. "Sheffield to Yarmouth."

"Yarmouth here, Captain Jenkins. Who am I speaking to?"

"Lieutenant Moore, sir."

"What is your status, lieutenant?"

"We are listing ten degrees to starboard and gaining, fifteen by the stern, no, it's now seventeen. CIC is gone, no other senior officers. Engine room is flooding and fires prevent evacuation."

There was a considerable pause. "We won't get to you in time, lieutenant. Seas are too rough to abandon ship. You will have to keep her afloat as long as you can."

At this time, James heard the near, haunting, and whispering voice of Hans. "The welfare of the many has to outweigh the loss of a few."

"Can you still hear me? Do you understand, lieutenant?"

"Aye, aye, sir."

James studied the display showing the ship's status, his eyes were heavily hooded, and the dried blood emphasized the strain, as his jaw clenched. The engine room personnel battled the fires as the water level rose, and Stephen looked on, the burden of understanding heavy on him but light on his unknowing crew.

"Get me whoever is fighting the fire into the engine room," said James.

Reade picked up a phone and then passed it to James. "Seaman Jeffries, sir."

"Jeffries, can you give me an update?"

The response was what he expected. It got worse by the minute and would reach a point where the flooding would make the next order impossible.

"Seal the engine room... Yes, I understand. I'm giving you an order. Seal the engine room."

The echo of his words and the sounds of dying men carried over into a waking sleep, and he sat up with a start, sweating and panting, to be comforted by Helen.

Chapter 26

Helen walked into the medical examination room to find a nurse and pediatrician kneeling on a mat in a cushioned play area with a boy of around twelve-years-old. He rocked slightly and looked away off into the distance at an obscure angle.

The doctor extended his hand. "Dr. Thompson, Michael Clarke, staff pediatrician. I thought you might like to see this for yourself."

Helen kneeled near the child and watched with interest. "Nice to meet you, and please, it's Helen."

"I have seen this happen before - it is quite remarkable. He is running a high fever, and for reasons unknown, the children often become quite lucid and communicative... ask a question?"

"What's his name?"

Before the pediatrician could answer, the boy picked up a nearby pencil and pad and wrote, not unintelligibly, 'Freidrich,' passed it to Helen, and smiled cheekily.

Taken aback by his awareness, she paused for a moment before responding. "My name is Helen, I'm here, Friedrich?" as she waved in his direction.

Freidrich wrote a long response on his pad and passed it to Helen, who read it aloud. "I can only concentrate on what I see, or what I hear, or what I smell. I am listening to you now and so I can't see you."

Helen sat back, a little stunned by this rare insight.

The pediatrician interjected, "A fever is a neuroinflammatory response. I believe this is proof their damage is reversible."

Without provocation, Freidrich spontaneously stood and spun around, flapping his arms, fluttering his fingers, and making clicking noises. This sudden burst of activity stopped as quickly as it began, and he resumed his position on the mat, quite close to Helen.

Helen decided to make use of this window while it was open. "Freidrich, why do you do that?"

Freidrich wrote out a response, and Helen read it out aloud again. "It relaxes me and I need to know I exist. I lose my body, my senses are disconnected. I only know I have a body when I am hungry, or when I get wet in the shower."

Their session was interrupted by the arrival of Hans and an aide, who took Freidrich by the hand and ushered him quickly out of the room.

"Dr. Clarke, you know the hive testing unit does not want his communication ability exercised."

"Yes, I'm sorry, director, but I thought Dr. Thompson would want to witness this unexplainable phenomenon."

Helen interceded, "Yes, I think it's significant, and I don't see why…"

Hans interrupted, softening somewhat, but still emphatic. "I agree, Helen, but the autism specialists feel it's counterproductive, and we have to yield to their expertise."

They left, and Helen turned to the pediatrician for explanation but he simply shrugged his shoulders. "The hive testing unit is isolated from us here in the research facility, and as you can see, they take priority."

***

The loading dock at the Savant Foundation was typical of its type, a utilitarian space designed for function and durability in which shipments were brought to or taken from this bay by trucks and vans. In addition to the shipping and receiving opening and ramp leading to the parking lot, it had a staging area and an office space for the dock manager and his staff.

Marianne was unseen, kneeling behind crates, holding a chimpanzee she had taken from its cage. Kirke entered and was immediately approached by the manager, who was, at that time, supervising two workmen stacking crates with a forklift. With little in the line of civilities between them, the manager handed over a clipboard. "Sign here."

"Where are they?"

"Over there, out of the way… what are they for?"

On hearing this question, Marianne tilted her head to hear Kirke's response.

"Experimental testing. We will sac them when we have completed our tasks."

"Sac? As in give them the sack? Fire them?"

Kirke laughed, a nasal whine followed by several snorts. "No, No. Sac, as in sacrifice them."

"On an altar, like?"

Kirke was getting impatient. "Don't be silly, euthanize them, then. But they will have made their sacrifice for science."

"Hmm… but they won't have much of a say in the matter, will they?"

Marianne listened and her eyes took on a blank stare as she remembered. She had been brought to the Foundation as a twelve-year-old, who had stared up with fascination at the ceiling fans as she and her parents sat waiting.

Hannah came from an office to greet them. "You must be the Dufay family, and this pretty little one must be Marianne?"

The father stood and shook Hannah's hand. "Yes, and thank you so much for seeing us."

Marianne's mother, who was dressed elegantly, almost fastidiously from head to toe, stood and paced the room as she spoke. "We have decided to go forward with the procedure."

"We haven't fully decided," said the father.

"Why wouldn't we try it, Andre? You will keep her here, is that right?"

Hannah answered, "Yes, and the cost of this would be completely covered... and, Professor Dufay, I understand you are having trouble securing funding for your own research. By chance, I think I have found you a benefactor."

Professor Dufay did not answer, but his wife did. "You see, Andre! We must give her to those who know how to deal with her needs, and I have been told that when she reaches puberty, we will be stuck with whatever we've got, for life."

"Kirke should never have told you that."

Hannah interjected again, "He does feel the theory is sound and gives a high probability of success."

"He's far too optimistic and is angling for his own funding. He's a former graduate student of mine, so I know his limitations."

His wife almost spat the next words. "We are doing this, Andre, do you understand me, I cannot suffer the embarrassment any longer with this freak of nature."

The young Marianne was dragged away screaming and kicking, attempting to bite the attendants as they strapped her down.

Hannah said her farewells. "You have made the right

decision, I assure you, and I will take on her case personally. She will be my protégé."

Andre and his wife left the foundation.

She was exuberant, he solemn. "You sold our child, you unfeeling bitch."

Marianne came back to her senses and walked out with cold determination from behind the crates and headed directly for Kirke and the foreman, a hand resting on her belt's tri-blade handle.

James happened to be walking down a nearby corridor and heard the high-pitched yells for help and screams. He ran in to the loading bay to find two workers high up on crates, their manager locked in his office, holding a bloodied forearm, and Kirke grasping the gate and holding it closed in a caged area.

Marianne paced back and forth, jabbing at Kirke's hands through the bars, as she yelled at all of them in French.

Her chimp was loose and on top of a crate, jumping, screeching, and back-combing his head with his hands, frightened by the violence.

James listened to Marianne's ranting over the din and approached her cautiously, and responded calmly in French.

"There is no need for them to use the animals for testing. I agree with you, it's inhumane."

Marianne turned, approached James, and stopped when they were toe-to-toe, her tri-blade pulled back and high at eye level, "Lie and you die!"

James didn't give any ground and continued with conviction. "Leave this to me and I will explain it to Hans. There is a better way. A simulation can achieve the same results, more efficiently, without this unnecessary suffering and waste of life. It's uncalled for."

Marianne's panting settled slightly to a more even rhythm, but her eyes probed James for deceit. He looked over at the highly distressed chimp, gestured for permission from her to approach, and walked slowly over, followed closely by Marianne. Offering his hand to help the chimp down, he was surprised when he took it, swung into his arms and wrapped his arms and legs around him tightly.

Lowering her knife, Marianne studied James with interest and reverted to English. "What's your name?"

"James, James Moore."

"You threw me into the trunk."

"Yes, I'm sorry about that."

"To rescue your girlfriend."

"Yes, my wife actually, Helen."

Hannah entered the area at a run and stopped in surprise to see the now diffused Marianne talking to James. "Marianne, come with me."

Marianne continued her assessment of James, while he noticed the chimp's name tag.

"Dino, now that's a nice name... Hello, Dino!"

Sheathing her blade, she extended her hand to Dino who took it and shook it in an exaggerated way.

James laughed, "Now that's what I call good manners, he must be an Englishman!"

Marianne smiled and stroked Dino's head lovingly.

Hannah repeated sternly, "Marianne, we have work to do."

Captivated, she still ignored Hannah. "My name is Marianne."

"Nice to meet you, Marianne."

"You are a good man, no?"

"I would like to hope so."

Chapter 27

James and Helen strolled past the town hall and paused to take in the beautiful guild houses on the Münsterbrücke bridge.

Entering the Haus Zum Rüden restaurant, they were shown into the Gothic room with its wooden barrel-vaulted ceiling and stone walls decorated with medieval halberds and stag horns.

They chose a table well away from other patrons and spoke in hushed tones. Helen decided on Zurich-style veal and mushroom ragout in a cream sauce, and James opted for the same.

"Have you found anything James?"

"Nothing, you?"

"Nothing."

"How do you hide a database of this size and the huge amount of communications that would be needed to facilitate it?"

"You checked the PCs in the lab?"

"They're all basic, word processing and e-mails… Kirke has a high-end system but it's off-line and dedicated to the magnetic pulse system, and CAT scan analysis."

They stopped as the waiter returned to check on them, and then continued.

"What about Hannah, James?"

"She has a powerful laptop, but there are just not enough hours in the day for her to process the communications from that many people."

"It must be in this hive." Helen looked at James, his face was pale and gaunt. "You look run down, James. This is not all on you to fix this."

James smiled, not answering.

Helen was about to say more, and he cut her off. "I'm fine, darling. Honestly."

Helen looked him in the eye, persisting. "Aunt Rose told me all about it, so I knew… you saved the ship and the surviving crew, James, and received a medal of honor."

James smiled absently, rubbing his chin, unwilling to remember what he tried so hard to forget. "They had to die, so we could live… It hardly seems right, and I live in the shadow of it."

Helen paused, considering. "It was a very brave thing, James. You acted; many would not have."

They looked at each other, their eyes full of love, and James reached across the table and took her hand. "Years ago, in secondary school, a P.E. coach pulled me aside and said, 'I need a striker who won't buckle under pressure and pass the ball back, but use every opportunity, and take the shot no matter the difficulty, over and over again. I want you to be the striker, Moore, and do you know why?' I had backed up a little, intimidated as he came forward, pointing his finger at my chest. I said I didn't know, and he replied, 'because you are not afraid to lose.' I had no idea at the time what he meant, but I understand now."

"He was right. It's in your nature, James."

"I see that now… and that medal, the Distinguished Service Order," he said disdainfully, "hangs as a black mark on my soul."

***

The Savant Foundation coffee shop had sculpted walls, coffee bean-shaped light fixtures and rippled tabletops which gave the impression that you were inside a sack of coffee beans. Brass and copper accents adorned the coffee bar and bar seating allowed the patrons to watch the roasting process. The walls looked like etched cappuccino and latte-colored foam and were adorned with dreamy art. Warm-toned lighting gave a comfortable vibe, hexagonal tiles of a warm hue covered the floor and mismatched furnishings created intimate and open seating areas. James sat alone, reading a document titled *The Collective Mandate*.

Kirke approached his table. "We haven't been introduced. I am Doctor Anderson, and I am the lead scientist here. I understand you will be joining my team so I will organize assignments for you. Be sure and report to me before you do anything."

In muddy corduroys, a preppy sweater, and glasses, he seemed to be working a little too hard on this image of the aging intellectual.

James rose and offered his hand. "James, and your name is?"

"You will address me as Dr. Anderson."

"There seems to be some misunderstanding. I'm not here in that capacity. I'm here to understand the foundation's purpose."

"Nevertheless, you will report to me."

A few patrons collecting their beverages hovered nearby, eavesdropping. James studied this little man, his patience waning but still tried not to overreact to the provocation. "We seem to be getting off on the wrong foot, and I'm trying hard not to."

"The problem we are having is you not knowing your place. I am your superior."

"It would be difficult for me to see you as a superior, and I won't be reporting to you, Anderson."

"Dr. Anderson."

"In that case, you will call me Dr. Moore. We can then trade credentials, but you will be hard-pressed to beat a graduate degree from King's College, London, and with sixteen published works and over fifty patents, I believe I will win hands down… Now, do you wish to start again? My name is James, and yours?"

Kirke was at a loss for words and turned several shades of red as the anger built in him. An explosive laugh from behind developed into a guffaw, and Marianne was almost bent over double, unable to control herself. "You have met your match, you silly little man!"

Kirke turned with indignation and left.

Marianne studied James as her laughter subsided, and she asked to join him at his table. She was wearing a teal-colored bodycon dress that accentuated the contours of her figure showing a highly toned, athletic physique. "You are different, no?"

"I think we are all different - unique in our own way. That's what makes life interesting."

A gentle alarm sounded on Marianne's smartwatch and she removed a pill box from her purse, opened it to show two lines of pills alongside a date stamp, hesitated, and put it away. James watched this with interest and gave a questioning look.

She scanned him intently. "I thought all scientists were old?"

"They all started young, but some people are born old."

"You are very handsome, Do you love your wife?"

"Thank you, yes I do, very much so."

"I have no understanding of these things. I am a mimic savant. I can copy mechanical actions immediately on seeing them."

"Fascinating. Can you give me an example?"

Marianne nodded unenthusiastically. "If I watch a piano piece from a concert pianist, I can immediately replicate it."

"How interesting… Can you modify the piece if you wanted to? Adding in a longer pause, let's say, for emotional emphasis?"

"I could before, but the blue pills remove emotion." Marianne's eyes gave away an indiscretion.

"And yet you feel great affection for Dino?"

"You ask too many questions, Englishman." Marianne took his hand and turned it left and right. "You have nice hands. They are strong but somehow kind."

James smiled, "I've never had anyone comment on my hands before… what are the yellow pills for?"

Marianne stood up, adjusting her body-con dress provocatively, and appeared confused when James did not undress her with his eyes. "My father is a scientist too."

"Oh really, what is his name?"

"Dufay."

"I met him!"

"What did you think of him?"

"He seemed unhappy."

"I will kill him one day, but at this moment, he lives in a hell on earth of his own making, and that gives me a great deal of pleasure."

Chapter 28

The museum building was in the impressive French Renaissance chateau style with dozens of towers, courts, and a park on a peninsula between the rivers Sihl and Limmat.

James and Helen perused the exhibitions using the time alone to try and formulate a plan. There was a comprehensive collection of liturgical wooden sculptures and panel paintings, and it was here that Helen first mentioned it. "We appear to have a shadow."

They moved on to the porcelain collections and doubled back to the Armoury Tower and a diorama of the Battle of Murten to confirm their tail.

A door led them to a darkened corridor displaying stained glass and it was here that James studied the young man in his mid-twenties. They were alone together.

"You're not very good at this," said James, turning to face him.

The young man turned. "I beg your pardon?"

"If the idea is to be covert, you have failed miserably."

The young man became immediately flustered and stuttered, "I'm sorry, sir, I mean, Professor Moore, but I wasn't following you... well, I was following you, but I wasn't following you, per se..."

Helen felt for the young man's distress seeing sincerity, and no malicious intent, "what's your name?"

"Ferko, madam, I mean, Mrs. Moore, Ferko Kovacs."

James was still prickly. "Why are you following us?"

"I wanted to meet you."

"Why?"

He spoke to James deferentially, somewhat in awe, "I'm an engineering graduate from the University of Budapest. We used several of your textbooks. I still have them, actually. I value them greatly... When I heard you were here, I had to meet you, even though the hive unit was given strict instructions to stay well away from you and your wife."

James extended his arm with a smile, and they shook hands. "I could sign those books for you if you like?"

Ferko was taken aback, and bowed in appreciation, "Oh sir, thank you, I would like that very much. Please excuse my familiarity, it is strange, but I feel as though I already know you so well through your writings."

***

Marianne ran to intercept Hannah who was leaving the foundation, and called out, "Do you need me, Hannah?"

The driver opened the door of the limousine and waited.

"No, Marianne, we are having an off-site security meeting downtown. It will be quite tedious, I'm sure."

Marianne appeared despondent and troubled.

"What's the matter?" asked Hannah.

"Nothing."

"Are you taking your pills?"

"Yes, I think so."

"You will get very ill if you don't, you will slip into a coma and die. Go to the doctor and get checked. I need you to be at your full potential, especially with those two snooping around."

"I like him."

Hannah stopped in her tracks. "Like? Like should not be in your vocabulary. Did you take your blue pill today?"

"Yes."

"Go straight to the doctor and get checked, I can't have you out of commission."

"Okay... I don't understand him. Why did he help Dino?"

"Who's Dino? Oh yes, it's that damned chimp. I will deal with this." Hannah lifted her phone and sent a message. "Go to your dojo and work out, I've sent a message to your instructor." Hannah climbed into the car and lowered the window. "He's the enemy, Marianne."

Marianne toyed with her hair, looking thoughtful. "But..."

"But nothing. Go straight to your instructor, she's expecting you." And the car drove off.

The dojo walls were constructed of bamboo and sat on a concrete foundation. These bamboo screens were tied with precision to allow a small gap between them, so light and wind were modulated on their passage to the inside. This structure was in an enclosed courtyard with mature trees around the perimeter.

Marianne entered and immediately changed into her sports bra and leggings. An older woman of around seventy entered, thin and attractive, with a walking cane and a depth of understanding in her grey-green eyes. She looked out of place, more at home in the library or the woman's knitting circle.

"What has happened?"

Marianne jogged on the spot, trying to alleviate the tension, "I don't know, Miss Jean."

"You are in conflict, I can tell, withdrawal maybe. Empty your mind, become formless, shapeless."

"I am so sick of all this shit!" Marianne lunged at the woman with her right fist, a single, direct, efficient attack designed to reach the target in the least amount of time, with maximum force.

The old lady stepped aside easily and Marianne tumbled forward, appearing to miss by a mile.

"The best way to counteract whatever it is is to be fluid - react and adapt - you did not signal we were to begin. I will not tolerate disrespect."

Marianne twisted around and, closing the distance very quickly, attempted to deliver a roundhouse kick by surprise. The old lady appeared to have all the time in the world as she dodged the kick easily, lifting her cane with minimum effort to deliver a devastating blow to Marianne's chest, who fell to the ground, winded.

The old lady walked up to her and kicked her hard in the stomach. "You have not been listening to me. I'm trying to help you... at great risk to myself, I might add."

Marianne rolled onto her back and sat up, still writhing from the pain and gasping for breath.

"Remember, we are always being watched. Stand up now and mask the pain."

Marianne stood, marshaling her emotions. "I understand."

"What are the three rules of engagement?"

"One, study your adversary to know what they will do before they do it. Two, wait for the moment when you can use that knowledge to attack. Three, do not care if you live or die."

"The blue blocker stops you from thinking of others, the yellow stops you from thinking of yourself - that is what makes you a perfectly engineered fighting machine."

Chapter 29

A security guard disappeared through the double doors at the far end of the darkened corridor, the echo of his whistle still lingering. Three shadows hovered at an entrance to the hive and Ferko swiped his security card through the card reader. They were granted access and entered an empty locker room. Ferko opened a door leading to a utility room. "Through there and follow the map."

"Thank you, Ferko" said James, putting a hand on his shoulder. "We will not involve you if we are caught. I assure you."

"Thank you, Mr. Moore."

"It's James, remember!"

"Thank you, James."

In the utility room, James studied a terminal. "They're incoming text messages, coded. It looks like another version of the enigma code."

Helen had moved deeper into the area, systematically checking the labels on panel doors until she found what she was looking for. "Here it is. Security panel two. Isn't that what Ferko said, James?"

James joined her. "Yes."

Removing the cover exposed a four-foot square aluminum duct which appeared to stretch off into infinity. Conduit and cables lined the walls and a series of grills at differing distances, and on different sides, allowed light into the duct.

James slid on hands and knees through the crawl space, followed by Helen, pausing now and again to look at a note with hand-drawn directions from Ferko. After several turns at various junctions, they arrived at a four-way intersection which had an extra-large, downward-facing grill in its center, from which they heard voices below. Most of the conduits and cables seemed to exit the duct and head down from what appeared to be a critical node.

James crossed over the grille quietly and lay down opposite Helen, and they peered in. This bird's eye view afforded them an unmatched perch of what looked like a wagon wheel with spokes leading to four bee-hive-like rooms. The director was in the center hub, encircled by four engineers whom each had an array of displays in front of them and their own one-way glass window looking into an octagonal hive cell. The children were all in their seats with their aides nearby, and in the control room, the director paced from one engineer to the next checking status while watching the child through the glass.

Ferko feigned a stretch in order to gaze up at the grill, and on seeing the outline of two heads, he knew James and Helen had found their way.

The director lifted his hands as though he was about to conduct an orchestra.

"Okay, on my mark, cancel all receptive conditioning, and let's feed the input."

The lighting in the hive cells dimmed. The four children were now more visible, and the director tried unsuccessfully to conceal his excitement. "Ready… Three… Two… One… mark!"

The children's displays went blank and the coded text messages James had seen earlier appeared at the top of the display of the input child and scrolled down.

She studied these for a moment and then began to paint a beautiful avant-garde colorful digital bit-map image. This emerging image was then seen on the processor child's left display and he analyzed it for a few moments before writing database request codes which appeared on the memory child's center display.

The memory child retrieved the full biographical data on requested collective members, and through writing recognition software, this was converted to typed text that then appeared in the processor child's display.

The processor child's eyes darted from the input data on the left screen to the memory data on the center screen, and then an output code appeared on the right screen. This code was seen on the output child's display and a few random, sporadic telephone tones could be heard as the output child pressed keyboard keys.

"We have throughput. Okay, bring the output online," said the director with exaltation.

Several dial tones were heard, and in response, the output child rattled out touch-tone phone numbers and text-message sequences which started slowly and then built to a crescendo of digital symphonic sound.

The director turned to Ferko. "Case study an individual packet and follow it through to verify."

Ferko was the engineer for the processor child, and in response, we saw his displays go blank, and then up came an image of a woman, seen through her cell phone camera, with a date/time stamp and location of Paris typing out five-character code sequences on her cell phone. These were seen going to the local cell transceiver, then to the local exchange, through France's international land-line exchange to Switzerland, then to a local exchange to arrive at the Savant Foundation, through the conduit in the ducts, and finally to the control room. There, the codes passed from the input child to the processor child, bounced back and forth between the processor and the memory child, and then finally exited through to the output child.

From there, they followed the same passage through telephone exchanges, to a local cell transceiver, and then arrived as a text message on the cell phone of a businessman in Tokyo, whom we could also see through his cell phone camera. He studied the message carefully, realization crossed his face, and then he smiled with euphoric pleasure, pumping a fist in the air.

Chapter 30

Marianne woke in a sweat, rolled over, and sat on the side of her bed to gather her senses. It was four a.m.. Leaning back, she thumped the body on the opposite side and a young man sat up.

"Allez, allez!" she growled.

"I don't speak French, sorry… Can I see you again?"

"Cela ne sera pas nécessaire."

"I don't understand."

"Va te faire foutre, pardon my French… Go, go!"

He quickly gathered his things and left. Her bedroom looked as though you were in eighteenth-century France where the juxtaposition between the silk-draped four-poster Louis XVI bed and farmhouse plaster walls exemplified country chic. Silk taffeta curtains stood out against the cream-colored walls and tile flooring, and matched the vintage bedspread. The room had high ceilings, a gilded Venetian-style headboard, and hand-painted side-table lamps with handmade silk lampshades.

Alone now, she climbed back onto the bed and stretched out diagonally to occupy the whole width, falling quickly back into a fitful sleep.

'What are they saying and what does it mean?' The dream had a sequence of speed ramp images showing the young Marianne being tied to a chair and a helmet being strapped to her head. She could hear a hum, no pain.

Hannah and Kirke talked but it was unintelligible. She was then a little older, and a second helmet was attached, this one was strange, it made her scalp tingle, and they talked again but she could not understand.

'Miss Jean was talking, I don't understand. More martial arts videos and men attacking me. She kicked one and he fell to the floor, his nose bleeding. She cried inconsolably with short intakes of breath between sobs, wake up, wake up!

The carryover from her dream took some time to dissipate. Her bedside clock showed five fifteen a.m.. Wiping her eyes, she dressed quickly and left her apartment.

***

Helen woke James. "It's a tapping noise, listen."

"What is the time?"

"Five-thirty. Listen, it keeps repeating."

James listened for a while, and then took a pen and paper from the side table, and began to write.

"What on earth is it?" said Helen, turning her head to find the direction it was coming from.

"It's Morse code."

"What does it mean?"

"'Garage,' it just keeps repeating 'garage.'"

"We don't have a car - there's nothing in the garage."

"Stay here, Helen." James got up and pulled on a shirt and shorts.

Helen followed, and in answer to him, she turned and frowned and said with a smile, "Stop telling me what to do!"

James accepted this with a chuckle and they both went to the garage door.

Disabling the security system, James unlocked the door and opened it slowly to find Marianne standing there, impatiently waiting.

"Put off the lights and meet me in the closet." She stepped past both of them, and they stared at her in disbelief.

The large walk-in closet had a chaise lounge at one end and a chair at the other end for dressing purposes. Marianne had pulled them together, and, sitting on the chair, waved the two of them to the chaise lounge.

James was about to speak but Helen took his arm and gestured for him to wait.

Marianne looked up and appeared to be gathering her thoughts. "How can I trust you?"

"Trust us with what?" asked James.

Marianne glanced to the side, shaking her head a little, showing slight signs of disappointment.

Helen took the initiative. "You can trust us because nobody here really trusts us. They watch over us with tolerance, but we are never allowed to see what we want to, and so we know very little."

Marianne pointed to James. "I like him."

Helen smiled. "I like him too."

"Is he a good man?"

"He is the best of men. I was lied to and betrayed by so many, I didn't trust anyone. He always tells the truth - he is a good, kind, and gentle man."

James looked at Helen, touched by her words, and they kissed.

Marianne watched this exchange with intense scrutiny. "He is clever, no?"

"He is."

"If I had a problem, you think he could help me?"

"I do."

James leaned forward. "Why did you send Morse code from the garage?"

"They have not bugged your apartment because Hans wants to win you over to his way of thinking and so he has told everyone to treat you with, em… children's mittens."

"Kid gloves."

"Yes, that's it. They have drones circling day and night to watch your comings and goings, and that's why they gave you an apartment with so many windows. I read your file and it said you were a communications officer so I assumed you would know Morse code. The underground garage cannot be seen by the drones and it is easy to break into as it is not on the security system."

Neither replied, processing the logic of this explanation.

Marianne looked Helen up and down. "You are very pretty, are you the sort of woman nice men like?"

Helen tried not to laugh. "I don't know, James?"

"Yes, I love and admire her, and she is the sort of person I hope to be."

"I thought men were only interested in sex."

Helen opted to take this one. "Sex with someone you love is infinitely more enjoyable."

James tried to corral her back into the reason they had been woken in the early morning hours. "How can we help you, Marianne?"

Chapter 31

James followed Marianne through the labyrinth of subterranean tunnels, and without their flashlights, the installed lighting would have been wholly inadequate.

"How deep are we below the surface?"

"About one hundred feet."

"What is this place?"

"The Romans mined for chalk to build their early structures. There were over sixty of these abandoned pits and in 1860, a nearby convent converted a few of them into wine cellars as they had ideal characteristics."

"What is ideal?"

"An even temperature of twelve to fourteen degrees centigrade, sixty percent relative humidity. Do you want me to convert the temperature to Fahrenheit?"

James smiled. "No, that's fine."

"This temperature and humidity allow the wines and champagne to mature slowly, reduces mold growth, keeps the corks from drying out, and prevents the labels from spoiling."

"You are a wealth of information."

"I remember everything," she said despondently.

"Me too, but I have help."

"The thing you told me to collect?"

"Yes."

"It was where you said it would be, and you were right, I was not followed, whereas you would have been."

"These are long tunnels."

"There are just over eleven miles of tunnels connecting all of the pits. I come here when I want to be alone... No one can tail us without being easily seen."

They passed racks and racks of champagne and came to an opening where a table and chairs had been set for tasting.

Facing each other, James took out the Mind Link.

Marianne saw the headsets and recoiled violently, almost falling off her chair. "I cannot wear that, no helmets, NO HELMETS, please, please."

James stood up and went to her, taking both of her hands.

She was trembling with fear and there was a wild look in her eyes.

"Listen to me Marianne, I will not hurt you. But you must trust me as I have trusted you."

"How have you trusted me?"

"This technology is what Hans and Hannah want most of all. You could have taken it directly to them, but you didn't. Even now, I'm sure you could easily overpower me. I'm not armed, and you are." He nodded to her tri-blade.

She looked at him, still frightened, but listening. "What are you going to do to me?"

"This will let you revisit your memories, but in this case, see them and feel them more clearly, evaluate them as the adult you are now - I can witness them with you, if you would like me to."

"I would like you to be there with me," she said, taking her seat but not letting go of his hand.

"I am happy to help you... when I activate the system, the view of this wine cellar will collapse, and then you will have complete control over what memory you access. Try something simple at first, a recent memory."

"When we talked in the coffee house?"

"Yes, that would be good. Just so you can get used to it. If you bring us into the present time, it will shut down. Or you can squeeze my hand when you want it to stop."

"I will hold your hand."

"Okay, you place the headset on you, and get comfortable with it, I will put on mine." He watched as she steeled herself, and sat waiting nervously with anticipation.

James activated the system and their present view collapsed to show the usual set of lenticular screens stacked in chronological order.

There was a pause and James knew Marianne was adjusting to this inner space. He gently squeezed her hand comfortingly, and in response, she traveled back in time, arriving at the coffee shop. He felt her tense as the screen lunged forward and pulled them in, and then she relaxed.

He watched as the memory was replayed, and marveled once again at the enormous detail stored in the brain. Her emotions then came through and these were strange to understand. She was a little giddy, energetic, heated, and almost euphoric. James was confused by these, and then he felt her squeeze his hand tightly and so he shut it down.

"How was it?"

She didn't answer and wouldn't look him in the eye, and was flushed.

"Are you okay, Marianne?"

"Yes, yes, it is wonderful. I just didn't think it would reveal so much. Again, again! I know what to do now."

James was made privy to a sad sequence of childhood memories. Her mother was a self-absorbed, domineering, and impatient woman. Her father loved his daughter, but put up only weak resistance to the mother's selfish demands, ultimately capitulating.

Young Marianne had been given to the Savant Foundation and it was Hannah and Kirke who had come up with the idea to weaponize her using her mimic savant ability.

Scene after scene showed her exposed to martial arts combat videos and an older lady she called Miss Jean, had her repeat the sequences with adult male fighters. She was faultless, except when she hurt somebody or was hurt herself, and then she cried like a child.

Marianne played sequences in rapid order, almost building in intensity. She focused on conversations between Kirke and Hannah, and James assumed that these were the frustrating parts of her dreams - in this instance, however, they were crystal clear.

Kirke read a report to Hannah, "The child developed her ability after suffering a brain injury from a car accident in which the mother had not used a car seat. She was five, and after developing frontotemporal dementia, she began to display replicating artistic abilities like sculpting detailed clay animals and award-winning paintings after only one glimpse, and musical abilities to match that of concert performers."

Hannah looked on at Marianne as she sat strapped to a medical table with a strange helmet on her head. "This isn't working."

"It is working, the magnetic field is blocking the insula and anterior cingulate which is where we experience pain, and the anterior insular cortex which is the activity center of human empathy, but it is only when the field is present."

"Well, she's no use to me walking around with this helmet on."

Marianne jumped forward to another memory with Hannah

and Kirke watching over her again, but with a different helmet.

Kirke adjusted instruments. "This technique is called transcranial direct current stimulation. It applies a weak electrical current to the scalp through a pair of electrodes."

Hannah looked at the apparatus dispassionately. "Looks a bit Frankenstein-like to me. Will it damage her permanently?"

"I hope so, that's the point. We want a permanent condition."

Marianne left this memory behind and settled on another.

Kirke was in his office and Hannah came running in. "Well? You said a breakthrough!"

"I have it!"

"Truly?"

"Yes. We can achieve the desired results with chemical blockers. She will need to take the pills every day. But early results show it is entirely possible."

"Good… very good indeed!"

Marianne squeezed James' hand and he shut down the system. It looked as though she had been crying for quite some time, her eyes were red and raw and she looked exhausted. She began to sob, her body shaking.

James took her into his arms and held her. "It was barbaric Marianne, a heartless manipulation of an innocent child - psychological torture."

"Like poor Dino?"

"Yes, just like Dino."

Chapter 32

A three-car motorcade snaked along the lake shore road through fog banks toward the elegantly turreted castle rising seamlessly atop a four hundred foot sheer rock base. They slowed at the gatehouse and were waved through to cross the narrow road which accessed the islet over the drawbridge, and then entered the graveled courtyard.

Security guards quickly exited the front and rear cars the moment they came to a stop, and converged on the center car, opening the rear passenger doors.

James and Helen got out, took each other's hand, and walked in under close escort. They were shown into the great hall and two guards remained with them, hovering at no great distance.

The huge fireplace was ablaze with tree-trunk-sized logs, the stone walls were adorned with paintings of rustic medieval scenes, slender black marble pillars rose up high to support a coffered ceiling, and huge stone-framed windows topped by a beautiful four-leafed clover design gave a generous view of the lake and an ominous dark cloud cover.

Hans entered, followed by a maid with tea, coffee, and a mini-food platter. "I took the liberty of having a snack prepared for you. I hope you don't mind."

James and Helen stood to greet him with a handshake. "Not at all, it's most welcome."

"The dungeons here are quite an impressive architectural feat, I could take you on a tour a little later if you'd like. They are cut into the rock base of the castle."

James handed a coffee to Helen. "I believe they inspired Byron to pen *The Prisoner of Chillon*?"

"You are right, James. A little too romanticized for my taste. He etched his name onto one of the gothic pillars. It can still be seen... You are well, Helen, I hear you are expecting. Congratulations!"

"Thank you. I feel very well."

A pregnant pause ensued as both parties refreshed their beverages.

Helen decided to cut to the chase. "It was a bit of a rude awakening, to be honest, and it felt more like a demand rather than a request to attend. You obviously have something you want to say?"

"You are right, Helen, I'm sorry about that, but I felt we'd all had enough time."

"Time?"

"Time for due diligence, time to decide."

James put down his coffee cup. "I see, and so when you said to take all the time you need..."

Hans interrupted. "I have given you a free hand, and from an image I was shown from a concealed utility camera, I feel you now have a very complete picture."

James continued, unfazed by their discovered infraction. "There's still a missing link."

"And what's that?

"Why do you need us?"

"The two of you could dramatically improve the efficiency of the Collective."

"How?"

"The Mind Link."

Helen looked puzzled for a while and then realized, "It's Friedrich, isn't it?"

"Yes, our processor child."

James turned to Helen, confused, and she explained. "His language skills are improving, and that means his savant abilities are waning."

Hans walked over to warm himself by the fire. "You are right, Helen. You see, the original concept creators of the Collective knew that to ensure its success you had to keep the database concealed."

"So that's how you hide it."

"Yes, what better hiding place than an autistic savant child - even the host is unaware of what they have?"

James leaned forward. "But how do you police the people in the collective - what if one of them turns you in?"

"Every member only has two contacts, like a link in a chain. It would have taken you an eternity to find your way back to us, link by link, and even if you got close, we could easily sever the connection."

"And they communicate with you through text messages, an enigma code?"

"Yes, information is exchanged with the hive through coded text messages that are sent to an untraceable, randomly roaming number."

"So why do you need the Mind Link?"

"Maria submitted a detailed report on your ingenious device. A remarkable achievement, James."

Helen picked up the thread. "Ah, I see, the Mind Link would enable you to store and retrieve the database more easily - and you wouldn't need a savant mind, it could be anybody."

"Exactly! Collective communications would be a lot less

troublesome. You have linked the biological to the technological. We could load it from a host to a PC, process communications, store it in a new host, and then bleach the PC's memory. Easy and efficient."

"That's it, James! it's been nagging at me, but I see now... autistic children mind-link naturally, do you see? They record every detail, as we do, but they don't need your technology to access it."

James nodded in agreement. "I see, you're right, Helen."

Hans took advantage of their excitement. "Do you see what an asset the two of you would be... please, join me in this quest. You will never want for anything again and think of the contributions you could make. Our philanthropic budget is in the billions, and our scientific research is shared openly for the good of humanity."

James looked at Helen, the knowledge of a previously agreed decision passed silently between them.

"If you let us go, we will tell nobody of the Collective. You can check on us from time to time to be sure if you wish... but we can't have anything to do with this. It is cloaked in good intentions, but malignant at its core."

Hans recoiled, taken aback with disappointment. "But why, explain your reasoning?"

Helen spoke up. "We fear for our safety once you have the Mind Link... we also disagree with the premise that the rights of the individual should be sacrificed for the so-called good of the group."

Hans tilted his head, responding to the emphasis. "So-called?"

James chose to answer. "It's you who defines good or bad, essential or expendable. Don't get us wrong, the idea of the collective is one of those ideal concepts that really should work. But from what we have seen of your members, they have traded certainty for morality."

Placing his hands on his knees ready to rise, Hans said with coldness, "You will not reconsider?"

"The Egyptian pharaohs killed the pyramid designers on completion to conceal its secrets. The target reticule may not be on us now, but it would be sooner or later. You are functioning fine as you are, and we are sincere with our offer of not exposing your organization."

Helen emphasized the offer, "We will keep to our word, I promise you."

Hans rose from his chair. "I'm sorry to find you both so resolute. I'm afraid you leave me no choice."

Chapter 33

James and Helen were hand-cuffed with zip-ties and shuffled down some stairs and finally, through a storage room, into the damp dungeon of the castle. Two operatives followed them into this cathedral crypt with Hannah at the rear. Stout arched pillars rose up from the stone floor to support the ceiling, and they were led to one of these gothic arches and chained to it, where they sat on the slabs of rough rock making up the dungeon's stone foundations.

Hannah came forward and looked on at them with satisfaction. "You have five minutes to say your goodbyes, whereupon," she pointed at Helen, "you will be taken to a sealed room in one of the towers, while you," she pointed at James and smiled, "we have something rather special in mind for you."

Helen was resolute. "We will never give you what you want."

"We will see how long you hold onto that conviction."

James spoke calmly. "Our offer still stands. It will be easy to keep tabs on us, and we don't intend to report any of this."

Hannah waved her hand dismissively and called back as she walked away. "Five minutes."

When she had gone out of earshot, James turned anxiously.

"Helen, maybe we should just give them what they want and walk away. You're pregnant, my love."

"Hans believes he has principles, but these are easily ignored when he doesn't get what he wants. She," she pointed at Hannah, "has wanted to get rid of us from the start and appears to hold more sway than we thought. No, we need to ride this out, otherwise, we are redundant, and a threat... Listen, James, do what you do best. Get out of here and leverage our release."

"I'll get us both out."

"No, if you get free, just go. We stand a better chance if they don't have you. I will also try to get free, but if you get the chance, run." She looked at him sternly and saw the reluctance. "You know it makes sense, James. What did Aunt Rose say?"

"I remember."

They kissed when they saw the operatives approaching.

Separated, they were led quickly away and James twisted his head to get a last look at Helen before she turned a corner and was gone. He was led down a set of spiral stone stairs, deeper into the gloom of the dungeon's underbelly, and into a room with a circular stone opening in the center. A winch and beam were attached to an oversized bucket which hovered over the opening, and James assumed it was a well, used to draw water. On closer study, he noticed it was a capstan winch.

Hannah watched him covertly studying the environment, looking for some means of escape no doubt, and was quick to disillusion him of any such notion.

"This is an oubliette or forgotten room. You will be lowered through this opening into a sealed stone, cylindrical room where the walls are three-foot thick - there are no windows or doors and you will have only a toilet and a bed. A guard will be here at all times - meals will be lowered in and waste taken out twice a day, and since your mind is probably already formulating a plan, this opening is sixteen feet high, making escape impossible."

The guard pulled open a small door on the side of the oversized bucket and shoved James into it, forced him to sit down, and closed the door. Hannah was beside herself, almost gleeful, feeling a great sense of retribution. "Questions, Mr. Moore?"

"Yes, just one."

"You want to change your mind?"

"Oh no. My question is when this is lowered into the cell, what if I refuse to get out of the bucket?"

Hannah turned to the guard and operative. "Show him."

The guard swung the bucket away from the opening, and they both grabbed James' arms, pulled him out of the bucket, and pushed him to the opening.

Hannah lifted a hand and they stopped. "You can be lowered in or dropped in - it makes no difference to me."

James yielded on this point. "It was merely a hypothetical question; I'd prefer to be lowered." Returned to the bucket, he watched as the winch was turned and he descended. Once he reached the bottom, he exited, the guard said "Clear," the bucket was lifted, and a trapdoor closed.

***

Days passed and despair and hopelessness got the better of him. These conditions of endless isolation inside a windowless stone cylinder with just a bed and toilet, and no human interaction were soul-destroying. Water and food were lowered in twice a day, and when James had prevented the bucket from being pulled up by using his weight and the folding camp bed, they had simply thrown in the water and food and not taken out his toilet waste. After two days of this, he gave up this tactic and allowed the bucket to be retrieved unhindered.

He found pieces of charcoal littered about the floor and used them to keep track of the days, but with the trap door closed, it was almost pitch black, making it difficult to see his markings.

After three weeks, he fell into a self-induced holding state and stopped everything except lying on the bed and gazing up at the tiny shafts of light that made it through the cracks in this wooden cover.

This was cruel and unusual punishment and losing all sense of whether it was night or day, he dozed on the bed, living more in his inner mind. The trap door opened and the shaft of light was almost blinding. He saw the outline of a head but his pupils took forever to dilate and clear up the image.

It was Hannah. "Have you had a change of heart, Mr. Moore?"

"Would you mind putting that light out - how's a chap meant to get a decent night's sleep around here?"

Hannah did not reply, but there was satisfaction when he heard her say to the guard with irritation, "Keep this trap door open, and that light on at all times."

Chapter 34

With the light now illuminating his space, he reached for a piece of charcoal, approached one of the walls, and went to work. The first thing he drew, from memory, was the winch he had seen - it looked ancient. The rope was wound tightly around a drum, creating friction as it bunched together, which meant the pulling force was applied to the rope, allowing objects to be lowered or lifted with ease.

After a last glance at his rendering, he moved to the right. This felt as similar as when he would move across his whiteboards in the lecture hall and he called out his familiar instruction, just to complete the illusion. "You have fifteen minutes to take this down!"

A voice above shouted back, "I'm not talking to you."

James smiled at the misunderstanding. "I wasn't talking to you either, Bill."

"It's Dan, there is no Bill."

"You sound like a dick to me."

"There is no Dick, only me, Mike, and Steve."

"Okay, I must have got that wrong."

"I'm not talking to you."

James wrote the three names, and alongside Dan, put a check mark, and 'eight-hour shifts.' He looked up and called again, "What?"

"I didn't say anything."

"I beg your pardon?"

"I DID NOT SAY ANYTHING."

"You're late with my food."

"No, I'm not. Food is at seven a.m. and p.m., waste taken out at nine a.m. and p.m.. It's not for an hour."

James started a new stone wall and titled it 'Timing' and wrote everything down. "Now Mike is senior to you, that's why he got the best shift?"

"I'm senior to Mike, which is why I got mornings... I'm not talking to you!"

"Okay, I understand. I don't want to cause any trouble."

"Good."

***

James circled the room, studying his writings on the wall. It was a problem to be solved, and through long experience, he had discovered that all you had to do was find the trick, or to be more precise, the technique needed to solve the puzzle.

"It's simply a case of perspective, I just need to look at it differently."

For some reason, Carl Gauss came to mind, and he realized he was mind-linking thoughts. The folklore in the science and technology community was legendary and many of the entrepreneurs were geniuses and so, by default, highly eccentric.

The story that came to mind was when Gauss was eight-years-old in 1785 at his provincial school. The teacher must have thoroughly disliked his chosen profession and would typically assign a long-winded problem and go to sleep. It was their first day, and true to form, the teacher asked the students to calculate the sum of all the numbers from one to one hundred.

The majority began the laborious task of one plus two equals three, three plus three equals six, six plus four equals ten, and so on. The teacher barely had a chance to sit down before Gauss raised his hand and said five thousand and fifty. The bewildered teacher believed Gauss must have heard the problem before and memorized the result, and so he asked him to describe how he arrived at that answer. Gauss explained that the numbers one, two, three and so on to one hundred could be paired as one and one hundred, two and ninety-nine, three and ninety-eight, and so on. Since the sum of these pairs is always one hundred and one, and there are fifty pairs, the total is five thousand and fifty.

James knew he had to turn this problem on its head and see it differently. To use the facts to find a solution to a perfectly designed problem that on face value had no solution.

This burn rate exhausted him, and he felt an overwhelming need to take a short nap. It was as he relaxed that the pieces of this puzzle became more mobile and combined themselves into a new semblance of order.

He sat up quickly. "Got it!"

Chapter 35

The preparation needed to execute his plan was time-consuming and tedious, but the thought of getting to Helen motivated him, giving him the impetus needed to work hours on end. The other guards could not be goaded into communication as easily as Dan, and since none of them felt the need to check on a prisoner who was not going anywhere, he worked with a will, not worrying about doing what he needed to out in the open.

Thanks to Dan, he now knew when it was night and day, and although he had to estimate the time between nine .a.m and seven p.m., and similarly between nine p.m. and seven a.m. the next day, his internal clock was always autocorrected by their fastidious daily time keeping to the schedule.

He had not returned a stainless-steel spoon during Dan's shift, badgering him for more food and questioning his sloppy time-keeping in order for it to go unnoticed. The handle had been filed down on a stone to give it a razor-sharp edge with the bowl serving as a perfect handle. He had purposefully spilled his toilet waste on his returned sheets and blanket, again during Dan's shift, and with that as distraction again, he got away with keeping a sheet. This sheet had been cut into strips and braided for strength to create a serviceable ten-foot rope.

The final parts of the plan required information. Dan had been milked for more details, and he had written everything down. Dan worked a shift from six a.m. to two p.m., Mike from two p.m. to ten p.m. and Steve from ten p.m. to six a.m.. He needed to disable a guard at the beginning of a shift, but a bucket delivery was needed for the plan and this meant it had to be Dan. He would, therefore, be moving around the castle in daylight hours looking for Helen and that was not ideal, but there was no other choice.

"Jim?"

"It's Dan… you know, it's hard to believe we need to be super careful with you. I think you're a bit of an idiot."

"Hannah said they don't pay that well. You've probably got a crappy car."

"I got a BMW."

"Old though?"

"No, 2021 BMW 330e - plug-in Hybrid, all-wheel drive, midnight blue."

"Wow, nice."

"I'm not talking to you."

"I can't imagine someone like you has a girlfriend?"

"I have a girlfriend, and she's good-looking."

"Does she like obese guys?"

"You are a son of a bitch, you know that. I'm losing weight."

"My wife is in the north tower, and she said the guards she has are pretty buff."

"You got it all wrong. She's in the west tower, and I know all those guys. I'm in better shape than any of them."

"I'm sure you are."

***

The following morning, he was ready to go. He waited for the tell-tale mumbling sounds which signified a shift rotation. Dan had a southern twang which carried easily and after he heard the usual goodbyes, he gave a suitable pause until all was quiet.

"Steve, why did you say that about Dan? I like Dan."

There was a long pause. "What did Steve say?"

"Oh, hi, Dan... It was nothing."

"What did he say?"

"I don't think it's my place - I don't want to cause trouble. I didn't know you'd changed shifts."

"Listen, James. I've got a right to know."

"I told him I like you, and he said I didn't know you."

"What did he say?"

"I told him I had made a gift for you, and he wanted to know what it was. I said I wouldn't tell him, and he got nasty, saying you didn't deserve a gift, and he said other things about you too."

"What things, James? What's this gift?"

"I have it, I finished it yesterday and was going to give it to you today after you delivered breakfast."

"Steve's an asshole, so don't believe a word he says. What's this gift? Is it valuable?"

"I'd say so, it's a one-of-a-kind, an original."

There was a pause. "I have your breakfast here, I'll send it down."

"Okay."

The bucket came down a little faster than normal and landed with a thud.

James looked up and could see Dan's head peering in.

"Come on Dan - it's meant to be a surprise. I have a box somewhere, let me make it nice!"

"Okay, okay."

The oversized wooden bucket had four individual ropes connected to four metal eyes built into the bucket's rim. These four ropes combined at a central shackle knot and were then spliced together to make the main rope which traveled up to the winch.

James slipped his spoon knife into each of the four individual ropes, cutting them in turn until they all hung onto the bucket by a thread. It was compromised completely and the bucket was being held by four single threads. He then tied his braided sheet rope above the shackle knot and let the excess hang over the side of the bucket. Having finished with his knife, he stuck the blade into the base of the bucket, dead center, and did a final check - all was set.

Dan was getting impatient. "Don't worry about a box, it's not needed. Are you ready?"

"Yes, almost."

"Say when."

James took one final look - it was now or never. "Okay, ready. I hope you like it."

Dan didn't reply. The bucket was pulled up at a faster rate than normal and James cringed as it bumped into the underside of the stone opening before making its way through.

He heard the click as Dan locked the winch.

"What the fuck is that?"

James stood out of the way, leaving the center of his cell clear.

"What is that?" asked Dan again.

He looked up, waiting for the crucial shadow that would cross the rim of the bucket when Dan climbed in to retrieve the spoon knife. It didn't happen.

"What have you done? That's a spoon. You've made a weapon - who gave you that spoon? Oh, shit, that'll be on me. Fuck!" And then it happened, the shadow crossed into the bucket at a fast pace to grab the knife, there was a series of tearing twang noises, and down came the bucket with Dan in it, landing with a thud.

Dan hit his head on the stone opening on the way down and was thrown free of the bucket, ending up face-down on the stone floor. James leaped forward, flipped him over, and checked his pockets but he had nothing on him. He was semi-conscious but in no state to resist. Using his shoelaces, he tied his hands and feet and moved on to the next step.

Placing the camping bed on its end, he gained six feet of height and placing the bucket upended on top of that put him at about nine and a half feet. It was, as he imagined, quite wobbly, so he dragged Dan's bulk over and propped him up against the bed for stability. Using the now-unconscious Dan as a stepping stool, he climbed up the bed and onto the top of the bucket, using the wall to steady himself. His sheet rope hung down and he hooked it and pulled it to test its strength. It was attached above the shackle knot and felt solid.

"It's now or never," he said and swung out, rapping a leg around the bottom of the sheet rope. It held. "Thank God!"

Shimmying upward, he used his elbows to wedge himself into the stone opening, gave a final lurch, and rolled into the upper room. "I made it. I fucking made it!"

In an adjacent room, there was a table and chair and a small kitchen. On the table were car keys, a pair of sunglasses, and a handgun. He took everything, including the jacket on the back of the chair. An evacuation map on the wall showed the quickest way to exit the building and it led to a parking lot, which was where he hoped to find Dan's car. He pondered on this for only a split second and then looked over the rest of the map for the west tower.

Chapter 36

This part of the plan had not been flushed out and he couldn't decide whether to sneak around the castle trying to remain unseen or stride confidently to his destination and bluff his way out of problems along the way. He had taken the map with him and looked at it as he walked, and decided that time was of the essence.

The castle had an irregular octagon shape with two circular walls, more than twenty buildings, and three courtyards. He traveled along the high-covered walk which led to the apartments and arrived at the west tower.

A guard sat on a chair outside a set of large wooden doors, and he stood up to greet James.

"Dan sent me from the oubliette, they've got trouble. He wants you there. I'll take over here."

"Who are you? I've never seen you before."

"Personal secretary to Hans Langsdorf - you better get going."

"She's a woman."

"You're right, I remember now." James took out the gun and pointed it at his head. "My wife and I have been held against our will and I am ready to kill someone. If you want to volunteer, go ahead and try your luck, but I assure you, I will fuck you up." This last part was delivered with genuine rage and the guard unlocked the door quickly and stepped inside. "Give me your gun. Slowly."

Helen was in another room and came in on hearing the voices, not wanting to believe what her ears told her.

"It is you, my darling. I knew you'd do it." They kissed and hugged while the guard stood stock still, convinced James was out for blood.

"Are you okay, Helen? I have been out of my mind with worry."

"I'm fine, but by the look of you, they have been treating you badly."

"It was expected. I'm the one they're trying to break." Keeping the gun on the guard, he walked to an arched window and looked out. "Can you swim?"

"Yes."

"Take off your shoes and jacket. Give me your phone and wallet. It's safe to jump from this window, there are no rocks below. You should go with the tide to that far shore. Fight the tide and try to swim back to the castle and it will kill you."

"I will leave your things here so you can get them on your return. Do you understand?"

"Yes." He seemed reluctant to make the thirty-foot jump and so James shoved him. He landed badly but recovered and swam off for the far shore.

"We have about a two-hour head-start with your guard. My guard won't be discovered for another six hours. Come with me, I have it all sorted out."

Helen kissed him again. "Why does that not surprise me!"

James led Helen back across the covered path, and although they saw several personnel, they were all crisscrossing the courtyards, traveling between buildings at ground level. Finding his way to the parking lot, he pressed the unlock button on Dan's key fob and a car nearby beeped. They were in and away, with

Helen badgering James to go over the details of his escape.

***

After picking up coffee and food, they found an out-of-the-way spot to eat and recover. James had the shakes, and it took quite some time for him to calm down. He hadn't realized how tense he had been, and if the truth was known, he had not been confident that his escape plan was going to work. Helen did not chastise him for rescuing her, but it was a great risk and they both knew they had been extremely lucky.

"What do we do James? Any ideas."

"There are two hundred and seventy thousand people out there who will be mobilized to find us, and they are all in positions of power. They will try to predict our next move and so we have to do the unexpected."

"What's that?"

"I honestly have no idea… Do you?"

"We could go to either the British or U. S. Embassy. I would suggest the British consulate as I think the U. S. Consulate would be more likely to be compromised. But I'm not sure."

"You might be right. They will have every airport and border crossing covered. They will expect us to run, changing cars, and choosing unusual ways to get out of the country. This could be it, Helen. It is somewhat unexpected, I just don't like putting us in the hands of some unknown entity."

Helen watched him as he processed this idea. His eyes focused inward and although he talked to her, he was really talking to himself. She had been offended by this in the early days of their relationship as his first phase was to test the validity of the plan proposed, and it always sounded like a criticism – and she was sensitive to this because of the traumas in her past. Every possible outcome would be evaluated and then, once the premise of the idea was embraced, he moved on to how it could be improved. This phase had also struck raw nerves from her past, but she was used to his ways now and knew he was using every facet of his ability to devise the best possible plan. He loved her, and of that, she had no doubt. They never tired of being together and there were just not enough hours in the day. She was pulled out of this daydream as he was talking to her, and in this instance, he really was talking to her.

"I think you are right, Helen, it's a good plan. Our weakness is telling the truth as it sounds too far-fetched... A secret organization in which all of the members are stored and communicated with by a set of autistic savant children? I can already see the looks of skepticism."

"I think you're right. But what will you tell them?"

"I have another option that will prioritize us and move us up the ladder to the highest level in the embassy."

Chapter 37

In cliché tourist attire, they tried to disguise themselves. James did not feel overly anxious as he assumed the search would be at all of Switzerland's porous borders, and not in its capitol.

As they strolled the cobbled streets of the Old City of Bern, it felt as though they had stepped back in time.

In the center of old town, the Munsterplatz plaza, was surrounded by stone buildings with stunning facades and one could easily imagine the town's folk of old gathering to meet and greet in front of the Cathedral of Bern. Just before the stroke of every hour, people flocked to the clock tower to watch the mechanical puppet show initiated by a grandfather clock that had been built in 1530.

Set in its own grounds facing a park, the British Embassy had walls and railings enclosing the site. The glass frontage formed the building's outer skin, providing thermal insulation in the winter and heat isolation in the summer. This glass outer layer reflected the sky, trees, and surrounding gardens, cloaking its presence. They walked to the front gate and were asked to show their passports.

"My name is Lieutenant Commander James Moore, Royal Navy retired, and this is my wife, Helen. Shortly after arriving in Switzerland, we were abducted and held against our will. I believe that since I was instrumental in the design of naval warfare systems, they were trying to extract this information. I request immediate protection for my wife and I, and to be flown home for a full debrief."

The two guards at the front gate just stood there frozen, but a sergeant had heard the whole thing and took over immediately.

"I understand, sir, please follow me, madam. Armed escort!" he shouted, and two Royal Marines accompanied them. They were shown to the office of the secretary of the ambassador, and he listened attentively, saying nothing until James finished for a second time. Picking up his phone, he made a short call, and then replaced the receiver.

"Would you please both come with me? I've been asked to take you directly to Dame Margaret Rutherford."

"Is she the ambassador?" asked James.

"Oh yes, appointed by Her Majesty the queen, after being approved by the prime minister and recommended by the foreign secretary."

They were shown into an office to meet the ambassador. She had gray hair and reading spectacles on the end of her nose. She removed these quickly and placed them in a drawer as though she didn't really need them. Her outfit was too tight and gave the impression that she was holding on to worn-out fashion styles. Her shoes were clunky and the print too loud, giving off very clear grandma vibes. She was extremely well spoken and signaled for her secretary to organize tea. "This is an extremely troubling situation. I do hope the two of you are unharmed, by the way?"

"We are fine," said Helen, "although they were not at all kind to my husband."

"What rogues! I have asked Patricia Drake to join us. She is the head of security here."

Patricia entered and introductions were made. She was in her mid-fifties, had a short boyish haircut and seemed a bit haughty.

She wore flat front, tummy control dress slacks in a dark gray, and a white oxford blouse tucked in. "We have your service record, you received the DSO?"

"Yes."

"Very impressive. For your role in the Falklands engagement."

"Yes. We called it the Falklands War."

"Quite. Quite."

Dame Rutherford seemed anxious to move along. "What is the plan, Drake?"

"We need to get them home as soon as we can. I have chartered a private plane to fly them directly to Heathrow. We may change that to a military base if necessary. From there, you will be taken to Whitehall for a full debrief."

"How will you get them to the airport, Drake?" said Dame Rutherford.

"Well, ambassador. I have organized a bulletproof limousine with a Royal Marine escort to take them from here to the private airfield. I will go with them, and personally ensure they are put onto the plane."

The ambassador sat back in her chair. "Now that is a relief. Well, lieutenant commander, how does all this sound?"

"Good, very good. Thank you both. We are very grateful," said James, and he and Helen hugged with relief.

***

James had to hand it to this bookish-looking head of security, she had the entire operation organized in just over an hour. They were loaded into the limo in the underground parking area beneath the embassy and James noticed there were two escort vehicles with marines. The limo was of heavy construction and extremely comfortable with reclining seats, a small refrigerator with snacks and refreshments, and a monitor for entertainment. A glass shield separated them from the driver and Patricia Drake, but she spoke through a video link to give updates.

He wanted to relax but knew he would only really feel safe when the plane was in the air. Patricia activated her video link to say the drive time would be about an hour and a half, and suggested they lay back and try to get some sleep. They both thanked her and tried to take her advice.

James woke to find Helen fast asleep next to him. He noticed the two escort cars were no longer with them and so pressed the video link button.

Patricia came on. "Yes, Mr. Moore."

"I noticed we've lost our escorts."

"Yes, our vanguard car went on ahead to ensure all is clear, and the rearguard has fallen behind so as not to draw too much attention."

"I see."

"All is well. The plane is fueled and ready to go."

"Good to hear, thank you."

"Not at all."

"We are close to Zurich."

"Yes, it's a private airfield attached to Zurich international airport."

"I see. Thanks again."

He sat back and dozed, noticing Patricia sending endless text messages, and then sat up with sudden alarm, recognizing the text message codes were that of the Collective. He pressed the intercom button.

"Patricia!"

"Yes, Mr. Moore."

"I'm feeling faint all of a sudden."

Helen woke. "Are you okay, James?"

Patricia said nothing.

"Could you pull over so I can get some fresh air? I will not delay us for too long."

Patricia stared at him. "Nice try, Mr. Moore," and the video link ended. She spoke to the driver and he accelerated.

James tried the doors and they were safety-locked shut.

Helen looked alarmed. "What has happened?"

"She was sending the exact same codes the Collective use - she's part of it. We are not being taken to the airport." James was up and ripping off the inside panels of the car.

Patricia turned to see what he was doing through the glass and sent off another message.

"What are you doing, James?"

"I'm going to remove this refrigerator, short the car's electrical system which will bring it to a stop, and then use the refrigerator to smash through this glass."

Helen watched Patricia watching James, and saw her begin to look alarmed and this time resort to a phone call rather than texts, not liking how quickly James was destroying the car.

The driver turned his head in a panic, and Patricia must have snapped at him, as he turned back sharply to focus on the road ahead.

The refrigerator was out and James looked inside the gap and took out a metal rack from within the refrigerator. Reaching into the gap, he insulated himself using a rubber mat, pressed a corner of the rack against the positive terminal which connected to the refrigerator, and then pressed the other side against the car's chassis, looking away as it arced and flashed brightly.

The car lost all power, its computer control system was disabled, and it was carried forward only by momentum. Patricia looked panicked but this changed to a smile as she noticed a tow truck pull up ahead of them. The car came to a stop on the hard shoulder, the tow truck reversed back to get closer, attached its line, and loaded the whole car onto its bed. They were off again at full speed.

The bulletproof glass was impossible to break, and the refrigerator fell apart before he had made even the slightest dent.

James put it down and looked around the passenger compartment. He pulled out the back seats to see if there was access to the trunk, but there wasn't. There wasn't a moon roof as this was a reinforced security vehicle. Helen looked on, watching his mind go into overdrive, all the while feeling an impending doom come over her.

They were on the lake road and she could see the castle off in the distance.

She put her hand on his shoulder. "It's okay James, save it for another time."

He looked up and saw the castle approaching and searched frantically for a Forlorn Hope. Something must reveal itself, some option must occur to him - but there was nothing.

They rattled over the drawbridge onto the gravel driveway and pulled up in the courtyard in front of the large open wooden doors leading to the castle's keep.

Chapter 38

Hannah and a dozen operatives came to meet them and encircled the car. They were escorted into the great hall, a huge rectangular room which had an impressive high decorative ceiling, many large windows looking out at Lake Geneva, a raised platform at one end for receptions, and a centrally-placed hearth. This expansive indoor space was beautifully decorated, well lit, had window seats around the perimeter, and was empty in the center of the room but for the seats that had been set out for them.

They expected Hannah to be gloating but she was subdued and moody - they assumed she was still sulking about the escape.

Hans entered the hall and walked to join them. "In its day, medieval times, of course, this great hall was the largest indoor space most people had ever seen and was a perfect means for a noble to display his power and generosity."

James and Helen said nothing, and Hannah moved a little further away.

"I have set our sights on the two of you and will not brook no for an answer. My God, you escaped from an oubliette, man!" Hans laid out a set of large prints on the table, showing the detailed plans James had drawn on the walls of his dungeon.

"Look at what your husband can achieve with nothing. You truly are a talent, James… I say, we put aside our differences and work on a term sheet for our agreement. I can assure you, I will accommodate almost all your wants."

Helen answered, "No term sheet. No deal."

"Come, come, Helen. Please reconsider and talk sense. We can offer you a life fulfilled. Sail the world in a super-yacht, James, publish a self-help book, Helen. Come on you two, give me a challenge?"

James answered, "Let us go."

"Now that, I can't do."

"Let us go."

"James, we have you. Come now, accept defeat like a gentleman."

"You seem to underestimate my resolve. It will be your undoing."

"Oh, yes, and so you plan to escape again?"

'No… I'm exactly where I want to be."

"Oh, really?"

"Yes, I intend to stay here until I have destroyed you."

"This is so unproductive, and I'm afraid you are now just trying to be unpleasant."

James fixed his eyes on Hans, and the look was violent, almost savage. "Your last chance. Let us go or I will destroy you."

"This makes no sense, you are both being so stubborn – why? Have you the strength to return to your cell, James? We will not make the same mistake a second time. You'll be there to stay, or until you change your mind. Have you got that strength, James? Can you allow Helen to suffer alongside you?"

"A moment of courage, or a lifetime of regret."

Helen turned to James. "Exactly right, my love, well said."

Hans stood abruptly. "Hannah, please show our guests to their quarters."

Chapter 39

Six months later ...

James sat waiting, shackled at the ankles and wrists in an interrogation room with a guard at his back. He was thin, almost gaunt, his hair and beard were overgrown, his skin sallow and grimy, but his eyes were alert.

It had shaken him to his core to see Helen so vulnerable and distraught. He had a son, how was that possible? He had known Helen was pregnant, but nobody had told him they were going to have a baby. Hannah believed she had the means to turn this around, and she had been right. Hearing Helen crying in pain and seeing his newborn son had tipped the scales - it had all been for nothing, all that pain and suffering for nothing.

The eight by ten room had a solid construction with sound-proofed walls and security mesh covering the wall ducts. The door was windowless with a flush metal frame and it looked like a solid core, with no lock or handle on the inside, so it was controlled by a proximity card reader or key code pad on the outside. The ceiling was a solid gypsum board to prevent any ceiling breach, and like the walls, the ducting overhead was covered with a security mesh. The floor was a solid epoxy on concrete with a small drain in the center to aid clean-up.

'Nothing... I have to get to Helen.'

There were only four pieces of furniture inside the room - a table, a chair for the interviewer, a chair for the observer, and a metal chair for the suspect which was bolted to the floor and included a cuff bar to restrain if needed. A collection of interview recording equipment was against the wall on the table, and there were two high-definition cameras mounted high: one viewed James face-on and the second the entire interview room from the side. 'There must be a way, think.'

Light switches and a thermostat control must be on the outside of the interview room, there were two pressure-zone microphones embedded in the wall, and a duress alarm to report trouble to outside personnel. There was also a large, one-way mirror in the wall opposite the table, offering a clear view of the proceedings - it was flush, mounted with metal framing, and would provide a one-way view by keeping the interrogation room brightly lit and the observation room dark.

'I have to rescue both of them, come on, James, think.'

Hannah entered the room accompanied by Kirke, placed a PC case on the desk, her own laptop in front of her, and they took their seats.

"We found the system exactly where you specified it would be."

"Good."

"Well? Let's get on with this."

"There are conditions."

"You're hardly in a position to negotiate."

Kirke, who had been eyeing James' laptop case, took the handle and pulled it a little closer. "Hannah, I can easily work this out, we don't need him."

"Could he, Mr. Moore?"

James' body language gestured indecision, but his eyes showed quiet confidence. Hannah opened her own laptop, "I'm assuming you have some sort of security lockout?"

"Yes."

Kirke leaned over to Hannah and muttered, "I can get past most encryption systems."

"Could he, Mr. Moore?"

"No."

Kirke recoiled with indignation. "And why not?"

"Because you're an idiot."

Kirke was stunned into silence, looking first at James, and then to Hannah for support, only to be further insulted when she smiled.

"How does it work, Mr. Moore?"

"You'll get three attempts to enter an exact key sequence - do it wrong the fourth time and the circuitry will actually dissolve."

"I think he's bluffing. I've never heard of anything like that."

"Have you ever heard of a subconscious to conscious Mind Link technology?"

Kirke did not respond.

"You lack the vital spark. I have watched you. Coming up with something entirely new and unknown is an invention, whereas taking something known and finding a new application for it through strategic problem-solving and creative improvement is an innovation. A key ingredient needed for both of these is to be open-minded."

"That is exactly what I have been doing."

"No, you haven't. You work with simulators programmed with only what is currently known and so you yield nothing new. You simply change the way things look, which is neither invention nor innovation, it's simply... styling. Dressing something up to appear new."

Kirke stood up and stepped back, and was about to respond

but couldn't. Hannah waved him away, and he knocked on the door, looking up at the camera. It was opened, and he stormed out.

"A little heartless, Mr. Moore."

"It was the truth. He blindly fumbles in the dark, and that would be fine if he didn't cause harm and suffering - he needs to be stopped. I'm frankly surprised at your choice of lead investigator."

"In the interest of us being cooperative, I will take that under advisement. Now, let us not digress."

"I want to see Helen first."

Hannah looked up at the guard and inclined her head with a nod to signal that she was to be fetched. As the guard approached the door, James looked up to see his relative position to each camera and then looked away when he noticed Hannah watching his every move. He leaned forward and opened his case, removing the laptop and Mind Link headsets.

"I will need two items. A hemostat and a phonograph needle."

"Phonograph needle?"

James stopped and leaned back. "I saw an antique phonograph in the great hall."

Hannah was anxious for no further delays. "We will get you one. We have another seventy-eight record player a little closer in the Bernese bedchamber. I will have them remove the needle."

Helen entered the room under escort, dressed in a hospital gown and robe - she was pale, thin, and her hair lank. Falling into each other's arms, they pulled away, and tenderly checked each other for harm. James insisted she took his seat when she flinched in pain and put a hand to her stomach. Hannah offered the other chair to James and gave instructions for the needed items to the guard.

James was still concerned. "Are you sure you're okay?"

"I'm fine, it felt good to walk, I feel better now being with you." She looked at him, taken aback by his appearance and pushed back his hair, her face unable to mask the disbelief. "What have they done to you, my darling?"

"I'm okay, honestly, it's you we need to concentrate on."

They both turned to Hannah, and Helen snapped, "Where's our baby?"

Hannah pointed to the one-way glass. "Your child is in the observation room. If I give the order, he dies. If you attempt to escape, he dies."

The guard returned with the required items, and Hannah signaled for him to put them on the desk and leave. "Now, about these conditions?"

"The three of us are allowed to go. You can have the Mind Link on a lease basis. I will set it to do what you want, but if I don't access it every six months, or if someone tampers with it, it will self-destruct."

"Unacceptable, unless we hold your son as a safeguard?"

"No!" shouted Helen.

"Why would you need him? You can find us at any time."

Hannah looked irritated and smiled belligerently. "Rather than negotiate your terms, let me offer a new proposition stating my terms... I kill your son in front of you, and then threaten to do the same to Helen unless you capitulate."

James and Helen looked on in silence, the futility of their position made evidently clear.

Hannah typed more notes on her laptop. "Now, where were we?"

Reluctantly, James continued preparing the Mind Link

system for access. "Okay, that's it. It's ready."

"I'm going to have to witness this myself, Mr. Moore."

James handed Hannah the primary headset. She hesitated, passed it to Helen, and picked up the repeating headset. "You do it, I'll watch."

"What shall I remember?"

"I don't care… anything," snapped Hannah.

James took Helen's hand. "How about the morning you told Aunt Rose you were pregnant?"

"I see you're a hopeless romantic, Mr. Moore."

James didn't answer, just set up the link and when the headsets were initialized, he activated the system.

He watched as Helen closed her eyes and Hannah did the same. He knew what Hannah was experiencing and was not surprised to see her flinch. For Hannah, to lose sight of James and see what appeared to be a never-ending stack of lenticular screens with moving images and sounds in a darkened tunnel, was, at first, quite disconcerting.

She wrestled with the impulse to rip off the headset for fear of what James might do but, trusting they would not risk harming their child, she watched with fascination.

Helen transported them back to a particular point and settled on one screen that then enveloped them. The realism was overwhelming, to see and feel everything Helen was experiencing at that time was intoxicating - and then it stopped, the link was shut down by Helen.

Hannah was incensed. "What happened? The old woman started to say something and then it cut out. If you two won't cooperate, I will have to find a way to motivate you."

Helen looked plaintively at James. "But…"

Hannah typed further on her laptop, "But nothing, do it."

James took her hand, "Stay in for a while longer, Helen. Let her experience everything."

"Yes. Do as he says."

Helen seemed confused for a moment, and then understanding crossed her face.

Hannah's eyes closed again when Helen accessed the memory, but this time Hannah witnessed how time seemed to slow when Maria came bursting out of the front door, screaming.

She watched, captivated, unable to understand why Rose and Helen turned so abruptly in response to Maria, and why Helen looked with surprise at her phone.

James had intentionally muted Helen's view, and when Hannah finally realized what was happening, it was too late. She received the full force of the sound spike, uttering a garbled scream before passing out, flopping face-forward into the desk with a crack, and bouncing off it to land in a heap on the floor.

Chapter 40

For a split second, Hannah's mind tried to maintain its own internal brainwave frequency of thirteen cycles per second but the full blast of the ramping, pulsating, reverberating sound spike swept the same frequency band and her brain tried to synchronize. Her vision flashed with freeze-frame, film-negative images like a strobe light sending her into a synaptic shock and eventual unconsciousness.

In the observation room, the woman holding the baby watched Hannah spasm in a fit, lose all muscle control, and hit the desk on the way to the floor. James leaped up and pleaded through the glass. "She just collapsed, but she's okay - we've done nothing."

As Helen stood in front of the glass to reiterate their innocence, James flipped the table, kicked out a leg and examined the break, kicked out a second leg and this time got the wedged shape that he needed to jam the door shut.

The woman's body language in the observation room signaled indecision as Helen pleaded with the unseen person, "She's fine, she's coming out of it."

James whisked Hannah's laptop to the floor, and while pretending to try and revive Hannah, he discovered she had open communication with Hans, sending him virtual updates. He searched 'sound spike' and found the source application, entering Hans' direct cell from her contact information. Accessing the sound spikes settings, he adjusted amplitude and duration to maximum and pressed 'activate.'

Hans had the updates from Hannah on his desktop display, along with video feeds, but he had not looked at it for quite some time, his attention captivated with a newly-acquired and very rare timepiece he had bought at an auction.

Hearing his cell phone ring, he removed his eyepiece with irritation at the interruption, looked to see the caller ID, and answered. It was security and his demeanor switched rapidly from relaxed to panicked upon hearing the news, and he looked at his display in alarm to see Hannah down, James unseen over her, and Helen at the one-way glass.

"I don't care what difficulties you're having, if he has harmed my daughter, there will be hell to pay. Get in there now."

A beep signaled he had another call and relief took over when he saw Hannah's caller ID.

"I have another call. It's her, thank God... Hannah, are you ok?"

Hans had been sitting on the edge of his seat, and when he lost muscle control, he slipped like a dead weight off his chair and onto the carpeted floor. By a terrible twist of fate, his phone bounced from his desk to his chair, and finally came to rest next to his face. The endlessly repeating sound wave sent Hans into epileptic-like convulsions as his brain expanded and contracted in a skull that would not accommodate the inflammation, and he began to bleed from his ears, eyes, and nose before going limp in a dead, vacant stare.

James had found the keys to his ankle and wrist cuffs and freed himself.

Locking the phonograph needle into the grips of the hemostat, he scored an opening in the glass with the needle tip, tapped the center with Hannah's shoe heel, and the cut section of the glass fell forward as a solid piece to the floor in the observation room and broke in two. Whisking Helen up into his arms, he passed her through the opening and, sliding the leg-less section of the table through the gap, he used it to climb through.

The room was empty, the door open, and they both ran into the corridor, searching its length. At one end, Marianne turned in confusion at the noise and broke into a sprint toward them. At the other end, they glimpsed a woman with their child turning the corner at a run. James didn't need a clear view and neither did Helen, and they turned to each other and said in unison, "It's Maria."

James stepped in front of Helen to face Marianne. "I'll deal with her, Helen, you get our son."

"Okay, but please be careful!"

As Helen left, James backed away from Marianne, well aware of her abilities and she in turn seemed to hesitate in drawing her tri-blade.

"James, what have you done to Hannah?"

James was about to answer when he was clobbered across the back of the neck with a chair leg. Hannah stood there, wavering, nose bloodied and face badly bruised, but pleased with herself. When James staggered to his feet, dazed, she punched him full in the face and he went down again. Pulling away her fist and shaking it out to alleviate the pain from the blow, she yelled at Marianne to help and they dragged him back into the interrogation room.

Chapter 41

James lay prostrate against the far wall, still dazed.

Hannah stood over him and Marianne took a seat.

Hannah seemed to have finally purged her embarrassment at being so easily overcome and it was now that she noticed with alarm that her laptop was on the floor, open with the sound spike application running. She dropped to her knees, studied the display with a sense of impending dread, quickly disabled the application, and called her father on her mobile.

"No, please no... Answer, damn it... Please pick up!"

Helen ran with a slight sideways skip while clutching her stomach, her face grimacing with twinges of pain. As she turned another corner and caught the woman in her sight, she shouted out, her pain smarting her cry. "MARIA!"

Maria did not stop, running through the ancient vaulted dungeons and then up a medieval spiraling stone stairway.

Helen had ruptured her incision and blood ran down her legs, leaving tracks.

In the interrogation room, Hannah thumped her clenched fists into her knees, wiping away tears and shouting with frustration at Marianne, who stood mute and did not appear to understand.

"I told him. I told him, but he would not listen." Her face was contorted with sadness and anger, and she reached to the back of her slacks and removed a slim handgun from its belt holster.

James had recovered his senses enough to sit up, and with his back to the wall, he slid up to a standing position. He was bruised and battered and he stared as Hannah came closer and pistol-whipped him across the face with a lightning-fast backhand.

"You are no longer important, Mr. Moore."

The blow made a gash across his cheek, which popped open after a delay and began to bleed profusely.

"We are all important, Hannah, even the lowliest sparrow," he replied calmly.

Hannah shook her head incredulously and then, with spite, shot James in the lower arm. "I have no idea what that means and I don't want it explained to me."

James recoiled with a cry of pain, grabbing the wound and holding it tight in an effort to stop the pain. But then he steeled himself, lifted his head, and took several long and slow deep breaths. "Even Dino was important."

Hannah's jaw dropped and she shook her head in amazement. "Okay, you have me there. Who the hell is Dino?"

"The chimp I saved in the loading bay. His life was important."

Hannah spat with pleasure. "Well, you wasted your time there, he served his purpose and then we disposed of him. After your little performance, I made a point of destroying that chimp personally."

Helen dragged herself painstakingly up a steel wall ladder to the roof of the chateau. It was a dark, cold, rainy night with only a slight level of reflected illumination from a crescent moon. Her gown, feet, and legs were stained dark red with blood. Her breathing was erratic, her face gray and porcelain white, and she adjusted her balance continuously as she limped forward.

Pipes, conduits, and ducts crisscrossed the puddled and slippery slate inclines, and Maria was cornered, trying a last locked door across a narrow walkway.

Helen was almost unrecognizable and she yelled in a slur to be heard above the sound of the wind and rain, "Give me my child."

"You will not believe me, Helen, but I never had a choice."

"I trusted you... I loved you. You were like a mother to me. I don't want an explanation, just give me my child."

"Your father hired me from the start, and when I no longer wanted to deceive you, they tortured my sons."

Helen dropped to one knee but was up again quickly. "James and I have put an end to this. We have dealt with Hans and Hannah... it's over - now give me my son!"

Maria struggled for a moment with indecision and then started to make her way back. "Okay, okay." Knowing it was falling on deaf ears, Maria still tried anyway although it rang hollow, "I'm sorry, Helen."

Helen did not respond, and her cold stare was unforgiving.

Maria crossed the walkway as the gusty wind tugged at her clothing and whistled as it was redirected around the sharp corners of the building. She walked deliberately, holding tightly onto the baby, countering any loss of balance with her one free arm.

A misstep caused her to trip, and she slid under the rail and quickly down the roof's steep grade. A tearing noise was heard as her coat hooked onto a protruding gutter nail at the roof's edge, while her grasping, free hand gripped the gutter with all her might.

Helen screamed a guttural roar as she lifted her hands to her face.

Chapter 42

Hannah took a few steps back and slowly lifted her gun to James' face, relishing the thought of where to shoot him next.

He looked back at her with an acceptance of his position, but defiance in his eyes, bracing for the shot he would never remember. There was a quick jerking movement, a shudder, but he was still conscious, unharmed.

Hannah appeared to be frozen in time, her eyes glazing over, and then he noticed the piece of metal extending from her neck.

She dropped to her knees and released her gun in a futile effort to staunch the pulsating waves of blood with her hand, but it oozed out between her fingers.

Marianne sobbed uncontrollably, looking at Hannah for forgiveness, but Hannah's deeply puzzled expression only exacerbated Marianne's torment.

James watched as her body went limp and her face went to a blank nothingness as she gave up the ghost.

James was still consoling Marianne when they emerged into the corridor, and on, seeing him, two guards made a beeline for him only to be stopped short by Marianne who said, "Leave him!"

"I have to find Helen, Marianne." As he ran down the corridor, he called back, "Please help me, she should be in recovery."

Marianne turned to the guards. "Do as he says. I am now in control."

They hesitated for only a second, before following her order.

She called out a question as they left, with cold deliberation, "Where's Kirke?"

The lead guard turned. "In the library, ma'am."

Marianne entered through the large, double oak doors into the library. Kirke was relaxing in a winged chair, reading a book and he looked up as she entered.

"I prefer not to be with you alone, Marianne. You are unstable."

Marianne turned back to the door, and Kirke chuckled, "That's it, off you go, you sad little lunatic!"

Marianne reached up, locked the doors, and as she unsheathed her tri-blade, it made the familiar metal-on-metal ringing sound as the impact to the blade sent it into resonance.

***

Helen edged herself down perilously, slipping and sliding on the rain-soaked roof, and stopped with a thump at the roof's edge where she came face to face with Maria.

She was still holding the child with one arm and if it were not for her coat being caught on the nail, she could not have held on with just one hand. Swinging precariously at such an unprecedented height over black jagged rocks below, it was hard to stay calm and collected, but Helen had no choice.

"Pass him to me! Please, pass him."

Maria shook from the strain, but answered in a fatalistic tone coupled with honest affection, "I'm so sorry, Helen."

In a valiant self-sacrificing effort, Maria swung the child up to Helen, but a tearing sound was heard and as her coat gave way, her hand took on the full strain.

Maria's eyes widened with fear, her grip gave way and she and the child dropped with a suddenness that took Helen's breath away as her hands snatched fruitlessly at the emptiness.

***

James and the guards had searched the empty chateau from the bottom up and finally, a guard called out, "CCTV shows she's on the roof... this way."

James burst through a roof door access but stopped abruptly when he saw Helen on the edge, wavering as she looked down.

He called out, "Helen! Wait there, I'm coming."

She did not answer.

"Helen! Don't move - I'm coming to get you."

Again, she did not answer.

As he inched his way to her, he could see the anemic glow of her porcelain white face, her blood-drenched gown, and the tracks of blood running down her legs. Looking over the edge, he realized with dread what had happened, struggling to reach her now as quickly as possible.

"Helen, please, my darling. Please come to me."

All at once, she became aware of his presence, looking up sluggishly, grief-stricken in a near comatose state. Her eyes held his with a look of calm resignation. She shook her head slowly from side to side to signal she was unwilling to continue, turned, leaned out, and fell.

James' cry was choked off by shock, his face shuddered and he was brought to his knees by the heart-wrenching agony.

Chapter 43

Two months later...

James entered the Savant Foundation, clean-cut and casually dressed. The foyer was busier than usual, and loping alongside him with a thoroughly inefficient and seemingly uncoordinated walk was a leashed black retriever puppy.

Marianne sat with an aide helping her with physical therapy.

She wore a designer jogging suit and sneakers, accessorized perfectly as usual. When she saw James and the puppy, she jumped for joy, running to him and kissing him on both cheeks in the European manner. Dropping to the ground, the puppy leaped on to her lap and slobbered all over her, much to her enjoyment.

"You promised, James, and here she is, merci, merci!"

"You are very welcome, Marianne. I'm sure you two will become fast friends! You are making great strides. Keep it up, you are doing so well!"

She stood and looked him in the eye. "You saved me, and I will forever be grateful. Thank you, mon cheri."

James left the two of them heading out for a walk. Entering a control room, he found Ferko monitoring several mainframe computers with his team. On seeing James, he walked over, smiling warmly, shook hands, and they proceeded down the hallway together.

"Everything is running smoothly. It is so much easier to

maintain with your technology."

"Good, always call if you have any questions, Ferko."

"Yes, of course, Profess-... sorry, James."

He pointed ahead. "They will make all the decisions for the Collective."

"I understand. I will run everything through them... They are quite remarkable."

James and Ferko entered Hans' former office, and there was Aunt Rose at her easel, painting the magnificent view through one of the expansive windows in her usual messy tunic, and Aunt May sitting by the fire with a book, having tea.

Ferko reached out his hand, "Goodbye, James, Thank you for all you have done, and good luck... I'm so sorry this happened to you."

James smiled. "Thank you, Ferko."

Aunt May tried to launch herself out of the low-lying sofa, to no avail, and James kissed each of his aunts in turn.

"I'm ready to go. Did you want to walk me to the car?"

Rose took his hand. "Of course we do, my boy. How is the arm?"

"It's getting better."

At the entrance, the aunts watched James loading the last of his things. "You're not taking the Mind Link, dear? We don't need it anymore," said Aunt Rose.

James shook his head. "I have found I don't need it either."

Aunt Rose was a bit confused. "Well, if you do, let us know."

Aunt May reached up and took James' head in her hands. As he bent down, she kissed the angry scar on his cheek. "It will heal James, you just have to give it time."

James smiled sadly, but his eyes welled up with tears.

"I do wish you weren't going, but I understand... don't be

away too long, please come to see us soon."

"I will Aunt May. Thank you... I love you."

Aunt May could take it no longer and began to cry, kissing him again and again.

Aunt Rose rescued them, slipped her arm in his and they walked the steps to his car. "After Gerald died, my hours felt like days. Never have I felt such incomprehensible loneliness within myself. And so concluded a love story of a man whose life ended before his time, and a woman who was certain she had outlived hers."

"I feel nothing, Aunt Rose."

"Well, of course. Grief starts with feeling, but this feeling quickly exhausts itself, leaving an emptiness, and it is in that blankness, I stumbled on a greater clarity."

James stopped and turned toward her to listen.

"What was the point of it all? What was the value of all that effort? We spend our lives trying to keep our life going, and the life of our loved ones, and it is doomed to fail. We can't keep life going forever, no matter how devoted we are."

"Well, that's it. Exactly."

"But don't you see, you must see life for what it is, James, and love it just the same. You must grapple with it – not turn your back on it before you can make sense of it all."

"I have made sense of it and have decided to never get close to anyone else again. First Dad, and then Helen, I can't do this again."

"But don't you see? The happiness you had with Helen is part of the sadness you feel now - that's the deal, James, you can't have one without the other."

"Well, I choose safety from this point on."

"But is that truly living?"

"My memory, serves me far too well, Aunt Rose. I replay everything in such detail, it is unbearable, but something in me needs this pain."

"You must not reproach yourself, you did nothing wrong... Better to have loved and lost than never to have loved at all?"

"Poets and fools, just words, Aunt Rose."

"Our souls are made of the love we share. They say you can't take anything with you but that's not true. We are here to learn, James, and experience is a great, albeit brutal, teacher. These are the lessons that enrich our souls - painful they may be, but they form us and shape us. This is what we take with us - what we experience here enriches our virtues. Some people focus on the negative, and they take those vices with them. Helen had strong empathy, integrity, and devotion. She will take that with her, and when she decides to return, come back with whatever she left with... Now, I must not rattle on, you must be off." She kissed and hugged him, pulled back, and let him go.

James climbed into his car, looked with almost unbearable affection at his aunts as they waved, paused for a second to register the moment, and drove off.